Blurred Vision

Blurred Vision

Chris Botragyi

Acknowledgements

A quick thank you to my family, especially my brother and sister respectively, Karl and Amanda Botragyi, who have supported and helped me despite their hectic lives—I am extremely grateful.

Also, my fellow author friends who have taken the time to share, help promote me via social media and offer advice, I thank you all.

And finally, this book is dedicated to my dad, Sandor Botragyi, whom I miss dearly.

Contents

Chapter 1

The Room

A dim amber glow lit the cold room. Tom opened his eyes cautiously. Shivering, he tried to hug himself, his brown eyes straining to make sense of the dark surroundings. Goosebumps dotted his arms as the chill grazed his bare skin. A static crackle—the only sound—emanated from the long, barely glowing ceiling light. He coughed as the cool, yet heavy atmosphere burrowed down his dry throat and into his lungs. The resulting trail of breath snaked through the strange red mist that floated around the room, the two entwining together eerily. His 25-year-old limbs felt ancient, aching as he shifted his broad athletic body backwards against the steel wall; he flinched, hissing through clenched teeth as the coldness took him by surprise. He drew his knees into his chest and held them in a tight embrace.

'God, please help me!' he cried as memories suddenly came flooding back into his confused mind.

He rested his elbows on top of his knees, and gripped fistfuls of his dark wavy hair. His grip tightened as the images of his beautiful wife, Connie, flashed through his shattered brain. He scrunched his eyelids in an attempt to banish the mental pictures, but the pain was too much. Suddenly, his head jerked up as he heard a noise. Panic setting in, he looked around the room, his eyes frantically trying to focus through the bizarre mist. His manicured hands slipped on the greasy steel floor grating. He began to hyperventilate as his heart beat erratically, feeling as though it would burst through his grubby white V-neck t-shirt. He realised that he wasn't alone.

'Who—who's there?'

The words rang around the room. He began to slide his crouching frame across the wall, seeking a sanctuary to ease his fragile state. The shuffling sounds continued, becoming gradually louder, forcing him to move faster. He was disoriented; his eyes shot in all directions, like ball bearings fired from a machine gun. Patting the wall gently, he quickly found a corner of the room. He sat and raised his bare knees back to his chest. Squinting in the weak light, he could just about make out a dark mass twisting on the floor several feet in front of him.

'What the... What the hell is going on?' came a deep voice from within the haze.

Tom sat silent, wide-eyed as his body shook with fear and cold. He tried to stem the stuttered rhythm of his breathing, watching as the dark shape morphed into a tall shadowy figure. A cold sweat began to run down his face in thick lines, stinging his eyes into closed submission as they rode his good looks.

'Hello, is anyone there?' the groggy English timbre spoke again. 'Hello, can anyone hear me?'

Tom's left knee slipped out from underneath his arm, jolting and scraping across the floor. He pulled it back in with speed, now trembling even more. He watched the figure freeze, silent, like a petrified animal sniffing the air for danger.

'Hello, who's there?' called the voice. 'Is someone there? My name is Mark, Mark Bennett. I'm a Professor at Stanford University.' The Professor inched gingerly over towards where he had heard the noise; he too tried to focus his dark brown eyes within the solid metal walls. Swatting his way through the mist 'I mean you no harm,' he gently offered.

Tom's fear reached fever pitch as the shadow loomed larger with each nearing step. 'Help me, I don't know what's happening,' he said aloud as the dark mass edged through the haze, sending misty patterns curling away. He thrust his head between his knees, realising that he was trapped either way.

'It's alright, I'm not going to hurt you,' said Mark. His vision cleared as he got closer to Tom's cowering silhouette. He squinted as he crouched down to Tom's eye level; they both came face to face. His desert-booted feet became unsteady as the rubber tread failed to grip the oily floor. He placed his palms in the moist dirt, and stared at the quivering ball of human before him. 'It's okay, I'm not going to hurt you. What is your name?'

'My name is Tom, Tom Valentine,' Tom mumbled as he raised his head slowly, his eyes bulging in terror at the tanned face before him. 'What's happening?'

Mark looked upwards. 'You're English? Thank God.' He ran his fingers through his tousled grey-streaked hair, keeping the centre parting as he stroked it back behind his ears. He placed a comforting hand either side of Tom's wide shoulders, who in turn began sobbing from a heavy heart. 'I don't know what's happening, Tom. But it's okay now, you are not alone anymore.'

Mark could feel the relief flow from Tom's body as he exhaled, deflating the rigid muscular torso like a burst balloon. He squatted next to the younger man who, even though now calmer, refused to avert his wild, tear-stained glare from the Professor's own.

Mark leant back against the wall; he took a moment to adjust to the sensation as the cold wall penetrated his light blue cotton shirt. He extended his soft palm in a friendly manner as he formally introduced himself. 'I'm Professor Mark Bennett, though I imagine that you've gathered that already.'

Tom nodded back quickly as the tears continued to stream from his puffy eyes.

Mark pulled his hand back, and stared deep into the man's glassy eyes. 'What's the last thing that you remember, Tom?'

'My wife, Connie, she—' he sniffled before another noise interrupted them.

They both fell silent as they scanned the area in the direction of the moaning voice. Their eyes locked on to a large black figure that knelt on all fours to the right of the room.

The Professor pulled Tom by the left arm of his damp t-shirt as he moved to get a better view. 'Hello...? Are you okay?' he shouted as he once again staggered through the mist towards the dazed shadow.

As he approached, he noticed the navy blue military uniform and glanced downwards. The colourful square pins caught his eye as they glimmered in the low light. They lined up perfectly in five rows that stretched across the jacket's left breast.

'Who are you?' asked the figure in a gravel-laced American twang, 'and where the hell am I?'

'My name is Mark, and that is Tom over there,' the Professor replied as he pointed towards the wall. 'We don't know what has happened, but we're trying to work it out.' He bent down to help up the man. He gripped him by his thick arms, grimacing as he used what little strength he had to haul the bulky man onto his polished black brogues.

'General James F. Hargreaves, of the United States Air Force,' said the man, unsteady as his full weight tried to balance itself out. His blue eyes glared cautiously at the Professor's close face. 'Don't worry about me, there are others over there.'

'Others?'

Mark and Tom scoured the room before coming across another three people that lay strewn across the flooring. The mist hovered over the stirring bodies, clinging like a ghostly morning fog along the banks of the Yorkshire Moors. They helped them all to their knees, slowly dragging the bewildered forms to the other side of the room. They all sat together, untrusting, frightened.

'I'm Mark, and this is Tom. He was the first to wake, but we have no idea where we are. Can anyone shed any light on proceedings?'

The group sat slumped against the wall as the hour ticked by. They shook their muggy heads, desperate to clear the wooziness that blanketed their minds.

Mark stood up and placed his hands upon the cold, damp and sticky wall to steady himself. He began to pace slowly around the room, counting as he went, '1, 2, 3, 4…' His fingers traced the contours of the steel's composition, attempting to gauge its texture. The grip on his boots squeaked as his feet slid through the grime that seemed to ooze from the grating. 'Well, the perimeter of this room is about 160 feet, I guess…and I can't see any doors or windows.'

He removed his hands from the walls before rubbing his wet fingers together. Frowning at the now smooth and sticky substance that coated them, he raised a hand to his nose. His curious head jolted backwards as his face contorted at the unusual smell.

'This whole room is odd,' he said, glancing up at the light. At five foot 10 inches tall, he could just about scrape the ceiling with his fingers if he stretched. He balanced on the tips of his toes, extending fully towards the dull, inadequate strip lighting that lay buried within the ceiling. Looking closely, he wiped his fingers against the legs of his denim jeans. 'Hmmm, the structure is incredibly well designed. I mean, it's essentially a long deep groove of light.' He waggled his fingers close to the humming. 'Strange, there's no heat being emitted from the light.' His face wrinkled as he painfully pushed his height to its limits. 'It's just light. There's no sign of electrics or batteries, nothing. Whoever designed this is clever, the power must be sourced from a core structure somewhere.'

The others looked at him, instinctively drawn to his intellect. They watched as he pulled his shirt cuff over his hand and pushed it through the light. He smiled as the energy buzzed with a prickling resistance, while the others gasped.

'Look at this,' he enthused, 'it's a forcefield of some type.' He then pushed his little finger into the light. 'Look, it's pushing my finger back like a magnet repelling another magnet!'

The group continued to hang on his every word. His face beamed with excitement as the orange light washed over him.

He relaxed and looked at his sticky fingers. 'Also, I think there could be something organic around here. I believe that this liquid—or moisture—could be emitting some form of gas, causing this red haze.'

A voice spoke up from the shadows. 'Gas?! What do you mean gas?'

Mark turned and focused his eyes on the unnaturally blonde-haired younger man. The dim light glanced off his youthful face, accentuating a stubbled jawline as he approached.

'Sorry, I didn't mean to scare anyone, but I want to know,' he added as he looked nervously around at them. 'I'm James, by the way, James Jones.'

'Well, James, we seem to be in a 160-foot perimeter steel room. I think that this red mist may be the reason why we were all out cold; it might have acted as a form of sleeping gas—it would certainly explain the headaches and disorientation,' said Mark as he waved his slender hand through the reddish air.

Mark glanced at the black roots that lay beneath the 19-year-old's unkempt peroxide blonde hair. He thought how trendy they looked, before searching the small blue eyes that sat within their oval face.

'Okay, Professor, you know more than I do. But is this "gas" harmful?' said James.

Mark shrugged. 'At the moment I would have to say probably not as we were only put to sleep. There doesn't seem to be any damage to any of us, though don't take this as gospel—I can't be 100% certain.'

The General looked at each of them in turn before his authoritative demeanour took charge. 'I'm General Hargreaves, of the United States Air Force,' he said with fervour, 'and I agree with the Professor.' He straightened his uniform as he stood bolt upright. Even in a situation such as this, his strong military values took precedence above all else. He dusted down his navy trousers before proudly fastening the four brass buttons of his jacket. His cropped silver hair appeared white in patches as the low light caressed it. 'We need to find an exit of sorts.'

'I totally agree, General,' said Mark, scratching the back of his head. 'But can you see anything?'

Mark and Hargreaves took a wall each, and proceeded to search the area with their fingers, starting from where the group sat. They ran their hands over every inch of the walls—as far as they could reach—in a desperate hunt for any clues to an opening. Step by step they carefully made their way around, occasionally slipping in the grease and stumbling in the poor light. Their search brought them shoulder to shoulder with a startling bump as they met in the middle of the stretch of wall.

'Got it,' said Hargreaves. 'Look, here, it's almost seamless.'

Mark's eyes followed the General's ageing hands as they settled on a set of parallel eight-feet high vertical lines. With his thick finger tips, Hargreaves traced out the inconspicuous grooves. He dug his nails into the narrow lines, and let his fingers continue their way up the wall.

'This has to be it, don't ask me how it works though,' he said gruffly. 'Looks like a sliding door to me.' He attempted to force the door sideways. He used all of his strength that was packaged into his stocky build, but gave up as the exertion filled his face with bulging veins and turned the colour of his skin claret.

'It's no use, General.' Mark itched his day-old stubble. 'You're right though. If it's a mechanical sliding door then there should be some type of control panel.'

'Like this?' said another male voice.

They both turned and stared as a slim man strode through the mist. His long finger pointed to a small two-inch charcoal triangle fixed next to the right of the "door", six feet up the wall. The three of them moved their heads closer, staring with tight eyes at the peculiar carved markings that adorned the shape.

'Well done—' Mark paused with an embarrassed grin as he realised that he didn't know the long dark-haired man's name.

'John Chapman. It's okay, Professor, even I wouldn't notice me,' he said lowering his face. 'Do you think that they're buttons, like on an elevator for example?'

Mark looked directly into John's chestnut coloured eyes, the fear all too familiar. 'Could be, John. But whatever language this is carved in,

well, I've never seen anything like it before—not that I'm an expert.'
He turned to Hargreaves. 'Have you, General?'

Hargreaves remained quiet.

Tom suddenly leapt to his feet and ran towards the wall. 'Let me out!
Let me out!' he screamed while simultaneously pounding the walls
with his strong hands.

The heavy clanging reverberated around the room. Mark and John
grabbed hold of Tom by his shoulders, struggling as the hysterical
man's athletic build suddenly became utilised. Hargreaves moved in
to end the conflict. He grabbed at Tom's t-shirt swinging the muscular
man off balance.

BANG, BANG, BANG, BANG!

The room fell into complete silence. James slowly moved out of the
shadows, followed by a thin man with short brown hair.

The whites of John's eyes glowed in the bleak light. 'What the fuck
was that?' he said as they all looked to each other.

Tom began whimpering as his eyes filled with dread. The grief-
stricken man clutched at Mark's wrist tightly—painfully—and pulled
hard. He thrust his crazed face into the Professor's eye line, quietly
pleading for safety.

'Shhh!' whispered Hargreaves with a rigid finger held against his
thin lips.

A few minutes had passed before their anxieties had calmed. They
all stood together, peering through the haze at the grim walls around
them.

'This isn't right,' said Mark as they began moving back from the
doorway.

'Help us, we're in here!' shouted John at the top of his voice.

Mark put his hands on his head and looked at John in horror. 'Christ,
keep your voice down!'

'Yeah, but there's others out there,' said John, equally as loud.

Hargreaves clenched his yellowing teeth. 'Zip your bloody mouth,
boy. We don't know who's on the other side.'

Blonde-haired James grasped the thin stranger's arm, who responded with a similar nervous grasp.

'General, what are you doing?' asked Mark in a tentative voice.

Hargreaves held his left hand up and signalled for quiet. His face creased as he leant his ear to the damp wall, laying it flat against the steel grooves. 'Do you hear that?'

The triangle's carvings instantly lit up into a red neon brightness.

'General, the triangle!' shouted John as he pointed towards the panel.

The grooves in the wall began to fill with a white light that ran through them like liquid. Hargreaves' face shot back from the steel as the light completed its cycle. A large slab of the wall opened with force; everyone jumped at the movement. The General zig-zagged several feet backwards, stunned by the sudden action.

Standing in the doorway were two seven-feet-tall grey beings. Their massive black eyes glared intimidatingly down upon the trembling humans. The mist circled them before slowly clearing and revealing their full appearance.

Terrified screams reverberated the walls. Mark and John grabbed hold of the General's arms to steady him as he scrambled away from the creatures. The three of them barely managed to stay on their feet as they skidded through the grime.

The aliens' thin mouths tightened as they bent down and reached out with long wrinkly arms. Enormous, bulb-shaped heads hovered closer as the humans shouted and cried, huddling each other as they were shepherded into the corner like cattle. With nowhere to go, they all fell to the floor and covered their heads with shaking arms.

Stay where you are—or die!

The words entered each of the humans' minds simultaneously, echoing around their skulls. Hargreaves glanced up from within the tangle of limbs. A sneer curved the nearest creature's mouth. It thrust its face through the red tinge, and directly into the General's quickening paleness.

The group continued to cling to each other as the two Greys turned and exited the room with a stilt-like walk. Pained screams—human—could be heard from outside of the door before it closed abruptly. They all kept still for a while until they were sure that the aliens would not be returning. They slowly rose to their feet.

'Jesus Christ!' said John as he held his rough hands to his black hair, 'I can't fucking believe this!'

'Fucking hell, what's happening?' added the thin man, trembling as he looked at them, as though they knew the answers.

James walked up to Mark and grabbed him by his blue shirt, crumpling handfuls of the light material. The force took the Professor by surprise, pushing him back before he dug his heels in. 'What's going on, Mark? You're the expert, tell us why we're here!' he said, maintaining his strong grip. 'Aliens?! What the fuck!'

'I don't know, James. I'm just as confused and scared as you are,' he replied, trembling fiercely. He placed his hands gently over James' who, feeling that the Professor was equally as frightened, relaxed his grip on the creased shirt. 'I feel like I should know something, but I can't remember.' With that, he slid back to the floor and placed his hands over his head.

Emotion rippled James' smooth skinned appearance. 'Does anyone know?' he asked. His full bottom lip began to quiver. 'Someone must know.'

'I think I do,' said Hargreaves as his square jaw came into the pale glow. 'I think that we are on one of the extraterrestrial ships.'

They all looked towards him; his eyes had a sudden glaze to them. He took a deep breath and dropped down against the wall.

James narrowed his eyes. 'Ships?'

Mark cocked his head to one side. 'This makes sense, this is why we can't remember anything. It's because of the mist—it's all a hallucination. You see, some compounds within certain drugs have these effects on people. Obviously, they—'

He was cut off rudely.

'Yes.' Hargreaves let out a huge sigh. He rubbed his lined forehead with the palm of his shovel-like hand. 'Yes, James, you heard right.'

'Heard what right, exactly?' said John as his limbs refused to stop shaking.

Hargreaves addressed the group. 'My colleagues and I were interviewing an extraterrestrial being at Area 51, trying to get information regarding a potential threat to our country's sovereignty. Things got messy, then there was a bright light—and now I'm here amongst you... in this place.' He looked around, staring at the walls with a mixture of disgust and embarrassment. They appeared to perspire as the moisture glistened in the faded light.

'So, this is your fault that we're trapped here like animals,' interjected James angrily. 'And you're only telling us this now?'

He walked purposefully towards Hargreaves, skating to a halt on the floor as John stepped forward to block his path.

'Now come on, no one is to blame. This is an unforeseen event,' John said as he gently held the angry youngster by his left upper arm. 'How can anyone have predicted that this was going to happen?'

James shrugged off the light grip, irritated at the gesture. 'How can you all be so calm?! What the fuck is wrong with you people?'

'He's right, it is my fault,' said Hargreaves as he unbuttoned his jacket, allowing him to breathe more easily. He remained crouched, balancing his weight upon his aching feet. 'We were warned what would happen, but it was already upon us.' He stared at the floor as he stroked the top of his head in a calming manner. 'We should have acted immediately.'

Mark's expression changed as the General's words soaked into his brain. 'What do you mean "it was already upon us"?' he asked, perplexed.

Hargreaves lifted his head. 'Exactly what I said, Professor. We could have done more—should have done more.'

The group dealt with the events and admissions in their own ways. James comforted Tom, who sat in the filth, a crumbling wreck. He couldn't conceive the reality of what was happening around him. His body still shivered in the cold; the hairs on his arms bristled. James gesticulated for Tom to rub his arms in an attempt to get the blood flowing, but it seemed that his gesture fell flat.

The thin, brown haired stranger leaned with his back against the dank wall. His slim hands rested in the pockets of his baggy grey jogging bottoms. His cocksure attitude—a world away from his earlier terror—showed in his lazy stance. He removed his hands and nonchalantly began twirling the dark grey aglets that sheafed the lace of his matching hoodie. If he was still scared, he wasn't showing it.

John and Mark both stood. They gave each other a hard stare, as though together they were thinking the same thing—to sympathise with Hargreaves' predicament. John slipped his hands into the pockets of his olive parka jacket. He shrugged towards the Professor, letting him know that he was welcome to proceed.

Mark coughed, clasping his hands together to keep warm. 'So, who were the others, the ones who warned you?'

Hargreaves peered up at the Professor with burdened, bloodshot eyes. His tough personality dropped its guard, making him vulnerable, if only for a brief moment. 'Does it really matter? It was too late anyway. They lied, probably a trick of some sort,' he suggested. 'I'm still only remembering fragments at the moment though. I have a feeling that we are all suffering from a form of memory loss.'

'Who lied, General?'

'The creature we were interviewing was one of those bastards!' he snapped, pointing towards the door. 'It said that it was warning us against two other races, Greens and Blues or something.'

'What does that mean, Greens and Blues?'

The General rolled his eyes. 'Greens and blues—colours, Professor!' He looked back at the door. 'Think about it, those freaks are grey. It was all misdirection.'

'Misdirection, but why, for what purpose?'

'I have no idea,' said Hargreaves bluntly.

Mark stumbled over to Hargreaves, who shouldered the entire blame upon his heavy build. 'Nobody's to blame. Besides, what difference does it make? They are far more technologically advanced than us.' He lowered himself down next to the General. 'Yes, I agree, General, it would have been too late. But how do you know all of this? You've just said yourself that you're only receiving fragments. I mean, none of us seems to be able to remember anything.' A suspicious look crossed Mark's face. 'Have you known since we woke here?'

'No. Let's just say that when those "things" entered this room, it hit me like a brick to the head. Their faces… I remembered their faces.'

Silence dominated the room as they paced, pondered and hoped. James remained with Tom, his arm around the man's shoulders as they huddled to keep warm. Tom stared blankly, as though he had switched off. James turned from him, his own attention drawn by the strange mist. He sat watching, mesmerised as it curled within itself, almost alive.

Mark and John squatted next to each other again, their eyes scanning the room in an uncomfortable silence. John tried to gather the hem of his jacket as it brushed the dirty floor. Mark buttoned the top of his own shirt; he had noticed that another drop in temperature had occurred.

The stranger stood quietly alone as he stared at the humbled General. 'For Christ's sake, what's the next step?' he asked finally as he relaxed his skinny arms. He used his right foot to push himself forwards from the wall.

The others looked to him as his words woke them from their slumbering thoughts.

'That's a good question, friend. I'm sorry, but what is your name? I didn't get it,' asked Mark.

'Daniel, Daniel Lambert. I didn't get a chance to introduce myself earlier as there were, are, more important things to worry about.' He ruffled his short hair with his fingertips, and nodded towards Mark with dark brooding eyes.

The Professor acknowledged the courtesy. 'He's right, we've got to get out of here.'

'That's not what I meant,' Daniel laughed. 'Besides, how are we going to get out of the door, and then past God knows how many of these creatures? And all this ends with us getting off this craft?'

'Should we even try?' said James as he looked to Daniel, who again fidgeted with the cords of his hoodie. 'We still don't even know what's going on, do we?'

A gentle throb began to course underneath the steel grating of the room. They looked at each other with worrying glances as they tried to balance their body weight.

John slid his torso up the wall. 'Are we moving, or do you reckon we're static, you know, hovering?'

'I don't know. Might just be the propulsion systems that are kicking in,' said Mark as he sat on the floor. Yeah, kicking in to begin flight—or to end it, to land!

Tom whimpered as he rocked his cold body back and forth; he looked shot to bits as the throb pulsated through his body in nauseating waves.

'He's done in, don't you think?' said John as he looked increasingly worried by Tom's cracking sanity. 'I wonder what happened to him? He's not right, better keep an eye on him.'

Mark rubbed his chin with the back of his hand, itching his skin with the sharp stubble. 'I think that something happened to his wife, but I'm not sure. I would definitely say that he's getting worse though, especially since the aliens revealed themselves.' He moved his hand around to the back of his hairline. 'Something bad frightened him—hurt him.'

Tom's eyes projected an innocence, looking through them as they discussed his ever decreasing psyche. His left hand yanked hard on James' light cotton jacket sleeve, desperate for attention. With his right, he stroked the sweaty hair back from his eyes. 'My wife, my Connie,' he whispered in a hoarse croak.

James turned and felt Tom's warm forehead, guessing that he was feverish. His look to the others did little to instil any confidence in them.

Tom cried hard as the memories stung his soul. He pushed his head deep into James' arms, which tightened more with each heartfelt sob.

'You can remember your wife?' Mark walked closer towards the two hunched men. 'How?'

Tom's eyes peered out from the comfort of James' jacket forearm. 'My wife, my Connie.'

The Professor placed his hands on his hips, staring sadly at Tom before turning his own teary glance away. 'I'm sorry, Tom. To lose someone is awful, especially a loved one.'

He sighed as he looked to Hargreaves, who continued to glare at the dirty flooring, ashamed of himself. He watched as John fought his way through the haze, still shaking his head as he leant and patted the General on his large shoulder. This was not the time for blame as they all shared Tom's grief.

'Ahhh!' shrieked James, startling the others. A crawling feeling slowly tickled his fair skin. He glanced down at his denim covered calf. 'What the fuck?' A strange blue inch-long insect—like an alien version of a cockroach—had scampered underneath the right leg of his jeans, and across his goose bump-laden skin.

'What's the matter?' asked John, attentions diverted.

'Fucking hell!' James clawed at his trouser leg with urgency, desperate to flush out the insect. 'Don't you dare bite me, you little shit.'

Mark skidded through the mist, and tried to assist the freaked out teenager. 'Keep still, I can't help you otherwise.' He pulled James to his feet while trying to lift the denim over the youngster's calf muscle. 'Now shake your leg! Don't let it bite you, we don't know if it's poisonous. Shake your leg!'

The insect dropped onto his black woolly sock; the thorn-like barbs that protruded out from its legs caught in the fluffy material, leaving it dangling in a frenetic spin.

'Get it off!' James shouted angrily. After realising that it no longer posed any threat, he looked closer at it. His expression changed to one of hatred as he flicked it hard, sending it reeling to the floor. He walked over to where it crawled, dazed. A large black leather boot shadowed the creature before crushing it with force; pink guts exploded out from underneath the sole of his right boot. His mouth dropped in disgust as he furiously scraped the tread over the grating, desperate to remove the mess. 'Fucking insects,' he shuddered.

The commotion sent Tom into a frenzy. James was pushed aside as Tom ran towards the walls, hammering each one with his bruised fists.

'Stop it, they'll come back!' said Daniel through clenched teeth. He lost his cool. He launched himself across the room and lunged at Tom, punching him twice in the face until he quietened.

James confronted Daniel with a hard push to the chest. 'What the hell are you doing?'

Daniel slowed to regain his breath after the exertion. 'Someone had to fucking shut him up, I didn't see any of you lot doing anything!'

'Yeah, but that's not the way to go about things, is it,' interrupted John as Tom curled up on the floor, crying as he held his swollen left cheek.

'Are you lot for real?' said Daniel, his eyes widening in disbelief. 'You might have accepted your lot in life, but I haven't. God knows what they've got planned for us! I don't really want to hang about to find out, do you?'

'He's right,' said Hargreaves. 'We need to find a way off this craft, and now.'

'Thank you, finally someone with some fucking balls!' said Daniel as he clapped his hands sarcastically. 'Lead on, General, I'm with you.'

John looked to Mark with a wry smile, then back at Daniel. 'What? A minute ago you were the one taking the piss out of the others for wanting to escape.' He threw his arms outwards. 'Now suddenly you're in favour?'

'Enough! Now listen up,' said Hargreaves as he climbed to his feet. His 60 odd years had seen plenty of conflict—none like this in terms of the enemy, but the situation was one and the same. He winced at the effort before returning to his hard style approach. 'When the bastards came in, did anyone notice if they had any weapons on them, or anything that looked out of the ordinary?'

The group looked to each other, muttering amongst themselves.

'Out of the ordinary?' laughed James.

'I didn't see anything, why?' asked Mark, trying to keep tempers from rising again. 'What have you got in mind, General?'

'Well, it's a case of do or die. As we learned earlier, if we create enough noise they'll come running.'

'Then what?' interrupted James, 'we run out of the door?'

'Yes.' Hargreaves dusted down his sharp pleated trousers. 'Hopefully they'll have weapons on them. If we can get hold of these, then they will give us some protection at least.'

James' eyebrows curled into a mock frown. 'Great plan, General,' he nodded, rolling his eyes.

Daniel's long face contorted. He bit his bottom lip, baring his crooked teeth aggressively. 'Yeah, what have you fucking come up with, eh?'

'Superb! So when we run past the aliens—who, by the way, are probably not the only ones on this ship—then what? We take control of the craft and fly away, landing safely to a heroes' welcome? You fucking idiot¡sneered James. 'What about him?' He motioned with his head towards Tom. 'How are we gonna get him out?'

'Look, I'm not saying it's a foolproof plan,' replied Daniel, 'all I'm saying is that we can't stay here.' He looked to Hargreaves. 'Am I right, General?'

Hargreaves glanced up and took a deep breath through his wide nose. 'Right.'

Daniel approached the Professor. 'Mark, what do you think? Come on, what would you do?'

Mark closed his eyes. The voices in the room were causing his head to ache. He placed his hands over his face and sighed heavily. 'Look, I don't know what to do. I—just like you all—wish to get the hell off this craft, this we have established.'

'That's what I'm talking about,' replied Daniel in a cocky tone as he looked at them all.

The Professor looked at Daniel. 'On the flip side though, I don't particularly want to meet my maker just yet. Either way there's a high probability that we are going to die, but I'm in no hurry to speed things up. Besides, James is only saying what you yourself said five minutes ago.'

Daniel looked to the ceiling, discouraged by Mark's answer. He turned back to the General, who gave a nod of confirmation in his direction.

Hargreaves smiled, ducking to avoid the mist. 'Professor, I know who you are,' he said respectfully. 'We had been following your research very closely, and it was most impressive.'

Mark could sense a darker tone behind the General's words, a tone that suggested something angry was about to rise to the surface. He didn't like the way that the military man had changed tack. It felt like a personal attack was coming.

'Tell me, Mark, what really happened at Stanford?' he asked. 'We knew all about your findings, in fact we were about to ask you to come and work for us, but things went wrong at the press conference, didn't they.' He moved closer towards the Professor. 'Tell us, why was the conference cut short, and why the blackout?'

Mark squeezed the back of his neck with his right hand in an attempt to calm himself. He pursed his lips as the pain in his skull soared. He felt betrayed at the sudden assault. It was common sense that the military would know of any major technological advancements, he knew this; a lot of the work he had done over the years was probably under the military's funding anyway. He narrowed his eyes, sizing up the General as he tried to decide where this was going.

'What is he talking about, Mark?' said John as he turned and faced the Professor.

Daniel's interest piqued as he looked at Mark, and then back to Hargreaves. 'What are you two talking about? Tell me,' he said, intrigued.

They all stared at Mark. He felt trapped as the walls began to close in around him. What the hell is happening here?

'He knew what they were—he witnessed it first hand, didn't you, Professor,' said Hargreaves as he pointed towards Mark. 'Tell them. Go on, tell them what you devised, what you saw. Tell them why you refused to share your knowledge with the world.'

'I give up,' said Daniel as he held his hands up in mock surrender, annoyed as the conversation seemed to exclude him.

James raised his generous eyebrows. 'Mark?'

'I don't understand, General,' said Mark, confused. 'What are you talking about?' He began nervously twiddling with the white plastic buttons of his shirt cuffs. 'Bits and pieces, scraps, that's all I have.'

'You don't remember?' replied Hargreaves with a distrusting grin.

'Remember what? General, you're worrying me now. All I know is that I'm a Professor of Theoretical Physics at Stanford, that's all.'

'Hmmm… you will remember.'

Hargreaves and Daniel stood in one corner, whispering to each other. The tall man's head was tight next to the General's right ear. Paranoid eyes darted in every direction as the two of them conversed. Hargreaves held his left hand over his mouth to prevent the others from lip reading their conversation. Daniel's hands rose and fell in a series of constant gestures. The voices quietened as Mark approached them.

'What are you two plotting?'

Daniel looked to Hargreaves for approval. The General tipped his head with a brisk nod, suggesting that it was okay to talk.

'Mark, we can't go on like this,' said Daniel as his eyes shot around the room. 'We're getting out of here.'

'And how do you plan on doing this?' Mark scowled. 'I thought we'd been through this already, it's doomed to failure.'

Daniel straightened his back. He felt inadequate at Mark's intelligence as the Professor poured water over his fire. 'Well, what would you suggest, Professor? Like I said before, I don't wish to wait and see what they're going to do with us, do you?'

Mark glanced towards the ceiling. Why won't these people listen to me? The mist swirled around his head like spiritual hands, mystical and teasing. 'It's suicide! You could be putting everyone in danger.' He looked around the room. 'Look at Tom, he's not in a fit state at the moment. He probably never will be.'

Hargreaves cleared his throat with a gentle cough. 'Mark, wake up. By staying here and wondering what's going to happen to us, well, it's doing more harm than good. By the end, none of us will be in a fit state to do anything.'

'That's what they want, can't you see it, Professor?' interrupted Daniel with manic hand movements. 'That's the whole point—they're waiting for something. Perhaps the bastards are waiting until we're too weak to do anything!'

Mark knew they were right. By doing nothing they were pretty much signing their own death certificates. He admired their bravery, though it was pointless nevertheless. The fact that there was no proper thought process bothered him; he was used to thinking, planning. He wanted—needed—more time. But time was a luxury they didn't have, as he struggled to think his way through this; the problem being that his brain just wasn't working efficiently.

Daniel shook his head. 'Sod this!' Immediately he ran towards the door and began hammering with the balls of his fists. 'Come on then, you fucking bastards! Come on, open up.'

Mark tried to intervene to stop the madness, but Hargreaves clamped a heavy hand around his wrist, pulling him back.

'What are you doing?' said Mark through gritted teeth. 'Let go.'

The engravings on the triangular control panel began lighting up again. The white light shot through the frame's grooves following the glowing sequence. Once more the door slid open quickly. The group dispersed, running around the room like headless chickens, smashing into each other as they desperately tried to flee. As before, there was nowhere to go.

Daniel took a step backwards as the two extraterrestrials once again entered the cold room. Their massive heads broke above the red haze as they held tall; their eyes soaking up the fear exuding from their human prisoners.

'Now!' said Daniel as he made a break for it, sprinting towards the opening.

One of the aliens caught him by his thin forearm, tightening its grip with a spindly four-fingered hand. Daniel screamed as the pain intensified. The creature stooped down to Daniel's eye level and stared. I'll rip your arm from its socket, human!

Hargreaves released his own grip from Mark's wrist and leapt to Daniel's defence. His large build was still no match for the surprisingly strong being. The other Grey stepped in, easily pushing the General to the floor as if swatting an annoying fly from its face. The others watched with fleeting glances, trembling as they inched backwards into the shadows.

Daniel's legs began to buckle underneath his weakening body. 'Help!'

Mark instinctively ran at the aliens, dodging the dangling arms and long legs as he fought his way towards his fellow human.

Seeing this, Hargreaves rose to his feet and joined the fight again. 'Grab its fingers, grab its fingers!' he puffed as they both struggled with the grey leathery arm.

Mark yanked on the creature's fingers, causing it to release a raspy whine. Daniel broke loose from the vice-like grip and raced for the open door.

'Run!' shouted Hargreaves before the alien struck him to the floor again. He landed heavily on the grating before rolling over onto his stomach, stunned. He laid flat as he raised his head, watching with blurred vision as Daniel's grey jogging bottoms danced their way down the wide tubular corridor. They paused for a split second as they pondered which way to run—they went left.

The aliens turned and looked at the door. Their spindly legs sprang into action as they sprinted through the mist after Daniel; the bounding steps clattering the floor with each giant stride.

The door shot back across. The lights on the panel turned back to their familiar charcoal colour, signalling that the door was secured.

Tom began crying hysterically again, hunching in the corner as James offered him comfort, though trying to quieten him was the youngster's real motive. The tears ran down and over the swollen lump that protruded from underneath Tom's left eye.

Daniel certainly caught you flush with those punches! James thought to himself.

'He's dead! I told you that this was a bad idea, General,' said Mark furiously.

Hargreaves glanced up angrily as he slowly regained his breath. 'Well, at least he got out of this room,' he said. He wet his fingers and started to wipe at the grubby stains that now clung to the knees of his trousers.

Mark shook his head. 'At what cost, General?'

The overpowering smell of urine and faeces wafted through the air. They all looked at one another, baffled by the smell until they realised that it came from one of them. Their eyes locked in sync at the side of the room. Amidst the haze, steam rose from the grating as James squatted awkwardly against the wall. His grey jeans were bunched around his ankles. A dark yellow and brown puddle began pooling outwards behind him, swimming around his leather boots before congregating around the rubber sole.

'What?' he said sharply, 'I sure as hell aren't going to piss or shit myself, things are bad enough!' James extended his middle finger and aimed it rudely towards the group.

'He's gone. Do you think he'll be alright?' said John nervously as he shuffled next to Mark. He raised his dark eyebrows. 'Do you reckon he has escaped?'

James pulled his jeans back up around his slim waist. The group looked at each other again as he made his way back towards them. A short uncomfortable silence followed.

##

John's face twisted as he pondered his words. 'Professor, do you think that he made it off the ship?'

'Who knows,' said Mark in a hopeful, higher tone. 'For all we know he may well have done so.'

Hargreaves rolled his eyes. He was obsessively trying remove the muck from his clothing, but failing miserably. 'Please, you know as well as I do that Daniel hasn't made it. You're the Professor, you calculated the odds of survival from the start and let's be honest, it's not rocket science is it. There's no way Daniel has gotten off this craft.'

'Yes, General, but you never—'

'Okay, let's do this. Say for example that he got to the end of the corridor. Then miraculously, he evaded every Grey on this ship before finding a door out of which he jumped—with no parachute—from God knows how many thousands of feet up in the air.' His throaty chuckle struck the metallic walls. 'Really?'

Mark's facial expression changed. 'Are you for real, General? You and Daniel were the ones that put this whole cock-a-hoop plan into action, and now you're the one berating him for trying?' A lightbulb lit up in Mark's head as Hargreaves suddenly averted his steely gaze. The puzzle began slotting into place. 'No, please don't tell me that you planned this.'

'I don't know what you are talking about, Professor,' replied Hargreaves.

'You sick bastard, you devised this, didn't you? You encouraged him to run so you could test the waters for yourself, to test the threat so to speak.'

The others began to look at Hargreaves and take notice—they didn't like what they were hearing.

'We're never getting out of here, are we?' said Tom suddenly, resigned to the fact.

Mark knew that Hargreaves was right. Testing the aliens' security was a necessity, but not at the expense of one of their own. Surely there could have been an easier solution? Add to this the General's underhanded tactics, this wasn't doing the others any good. The Professor's expression said it all.

The ageing General gave a gentle cough. He got the point. 'Look, you all saw what Daniel was like. He wanted off this ship, and there was nothing we could have done. To use him in this way didn't make any difference, he was going no matter what.' Hargreaves straightened his torso and pushed his feet together. 'I take full responsibility.'

'You're damned right you do!' said Mark with a sarcastic chuckle. 'Who are you going to sacrifice next... me, John, Tom?'

John came between them. 'But where are the military, General?' he asked through quivering lips.

Hargreaves shifted a little uneasily on his feet as the group seemed to encircle him. He remained solid, firm.

'General?' Mark echoed.

'The world's militaries can't engage the enemy anymore, that's if this has gone that far, we don't know this for sure. If it has? Well, they'd be too strong and far more technologically advanced, it would be useless to continue fighting; we would no doubt have lost far too many men and women already.' The dull glow smothered Hargreaves' deep features as he looked at each of them. 'Besides, I don't wish to comment further on the matter, walls have ears if you catch my drift.' He searched his pockets for a cigarette, but to no avail. 'Does anyone smoke? I seem to have lost my cigarettes.'

James pulled his black sweatshirt sleeves from underneath his jacket cuffs. 'I was going to ask the same question, General,' he said as he covered his cold hands with the fleecy material. 'Mine are also gone.'

'Perhaps they like to smoke after sex?' said Tom bizarrely.

They all stared at him, unsure whether the words were that of a completely insane man or not.

'Forget that for a moment,' said Mark as he looked at Tom, then back to the others. 'How do you know that the military isn't out there now fighting for us?'

The strangeness of Tom's remark still remained as Hargreaves puffed out his cheeks. 'They could be, but one thing I can tell you is that we have to be smart. We can't throw people to the wolves for the sake of it, you have to survey the situation first,' he said with a sparkle in his blue eyes. 'Don't give up just yet.'

Mark stared back, just as bemused. Can't throw people to the wolves, eh? That's a bit rich! He narrowed his eyes as the thoughts flickered through his mind. 'You're hiding something, General. You know more than you're letting on.'

'Well, I hope that they find a way, and soon because this fucking smell is killing me,' moaned James as he wiped his greasy hands down the thighs of his jeans. He took in a deep breath through his small angled nose. 'I'm going to be sick in a minute.'

An hour or so had passed as the group sat, paced the floor, then sat again. It seemed to be getting colder in the room as they all hugged their upper bodies. The hunger was also beginning to set in as disgruntled stomachs grumbled.

The triangular panel began its familiar sequence.

'No,' said John, shaking his head as he pointed through the mist towards the expanding glow of the doorway. 'Look!'

They seemed to hold their breaths for a second as they anticipated the door's opening. The group shuffled backwards, trying to squeeze every part of themselves into the dark corners of the room. The door whizzed open. This time though, the Greys didn't enter the room. The humans waited for a moment, silent... nothing.

Mark stepped forwards into the haze. He could just make out the weak light that toyed with them, close to the opening.

'Mark,' said Hargreaves in a hard whisper, 'don't move.'

Silence.

The Professor looked back at the group's silhouettes. 'What do you think?' he asked with a confused shrug of his shoulders. He forced himself into a quiet slide against the side of the open door frame.

'Are we going home?' asked Tom with a glimmer of hope in his deranged eyes.

'Don't be foolish, it's a trap!' whispered Hargreaves, shifting his silvery head left, then right. 'Why would they let us go after all this time?'

The stench of rotting flesh wafted down the corridor and into the room. Mark raised his hand to cover his mouth and nose—the smell was awful. He leaned his left arm against the frame, careful not to be seen. 'You did say that you wanted off this ship? Now's your chance, General.' He watched as the mist exited the large opening in coiling swathes. As he stared down the empty passage, he could see that the same fixtures and amber lighting occupied the centre of the corridor's curved ceiling.

'Yes, but that was before they "invited" us out through the door. This isn't good.'

The group gingerly shuffled into the lighting, tip-toeing as they moved closer towards Mark's dark figure that stood the other side of the mist. His greying hair became more prominent as they crept up slowly behind him.

'This corridor is about 70, 80 feet long? If we can—'

Mark's words were broken off as Hargreaves sidled up next to him. 'Wait, we don't know what's lurking there at the end of the corridor, around each corner.'

'Yes, General, my thoughts exactly,' said the Professor, his annoyance obvious as he stared at Hargreaves.

Heavy footsteps rumbled through the grating, becoming ever louder as the sound echoed down the long stretch of light and steel.

'Get back, get back!' ordered Hargreaves as he hurriedly ushered them away from the door frame.

Frightened eyes peered out through the gaps in the mist as it ghosted past. Three aliens came into view at the end of the corridor, walking from left to right.

'What are they doing?' whispered James as his head bobbed and weaved, straining for a better look. 'I can't see properly through this shit.'

'Looks like they're carrying something?' said John, his head retreating back into the haze.

Tom began to whimper behind them.

'Shut up, Tom, they'll hear you!' panicked Hargreaves. He turned his attention back to Mark. 'What can you see?'

A human arm dropped to the floor; a glint apparent from something metallic that remained within the hand. Mark's eyes travelled the length of the limp body and wet organs, that culminated in two male feet sliding along the floor as the aliens dragged it away. Following behind them was the third alien, who held a dripping, ball shaped object in its creepy long fingers.

The Professor squinted his eyes as he focused on the scene before him. Two dark brown eyes stared emptily back at him. 'It can't be,' he said, turning away from the door. He placed his back against the wall, inside of the room. He looked upwards, clenching his eyes shut before opening them again, hoping that he was dreaming. The reality quickly returned. 'They're not letting us go—they never were.'

The mist crept eerily down the corridor. The door shut fast, cutting off the smoky haze, forcing the others to pull their heads back into the room quickly.

'Mark, what is it?' asked James, concerned. 'Why do you say that?'

'Because they wanted us to see it,' came the tight-lipped reply. The Professor ran his hands backwards through his hair as he looked to the ceiling again.

'See what?' James continued, frustrated. 'What did they want us to see?'

'Didn't you see what they were carrying?' said Mark, raising his defeated voice at them all. The shock in his face dragged his weary features downwards. 'It was Daniel, they were carrying Daniel—and he was in fucking pieces.'

Tom started shaking again. He suddenly screamed at the top of his voice as the realisation struck what was left of his sanity. He grabbed clumps of his thick hair and began swinging his elbows wildly. James swiftly moved to calm him again. He placed his hand over Tom's mouth, half stifling the cries as they both fell to the floor, their knees squirming in the grease as they fought one another.

Mark glanced at Hargreaves; his brown eyes swam with an intense seriousness as he stared deep. For the first time the Professor could see the fear etched on the General's wrinkled face. They each knew what the other was thinking.

'Why did he think that he could escape?' asked John as he dropped his gaze. 'He never stood a chance.' He pulled the parka jacket's hood over his head in an effort to mask his obvious distress. 'Stupid bastard, why didn't he listen?'

Chapter 2

Forced Hands—Daniel's Story

The glowing lights disappeared in an instant. Daniel lay there naked, dazed. He wept, as everything that had happened to him coursed through his mind all at once; it was a lot to take in, he was having trouble comprehending it himself. He climbed unsteadily to his feet, hunching as he embraced his slim torso to keep the cold chill at bay. He looked around to see where he was. A sudden, sharp pain forced his eyes down towards his right hand; a memory flash reminded him of being grabbed and thrown. A steam trail of breath rose into the dark sky as a rough cry left his cracked lips. His vision was hazy due to the tears that were corrupting his eyes. His throat—dry from all the screaming he had done—desperately craved moisture.

He couldn't stop shaking as a fierce wind shot through his wet hair. Every follicle on his body promptly reacted, standing to attention. The stinging in his hand intensified as the air pierced the deep lacerations that bled profusely. With his left hand he gripped the injured limb in an attempt to stem the blood flow.

The heavy rain pounded the road, reducing the visibility and blanketing the night. Passing cars scared the terrified man into an insane wreck as he spun left, then right; the jarring car horns were a cruel intrusion upon his fragile state, affecting his bearings. He narrowed his sore eyes almost to the point of closure. In the distance he could see several fuzzy yellowy lights advancing. His shivering body froze solid as the fear rocketed through his skinny frame. My God, they're coming back for me.

As the lights grew closer, so did the rumbling. Daniel silently cried out from his rasping throat, cowering as he shielded his face with goose-pimpled forearms. The lights became brighter, but the noise slowed into a gentle throbbing. Cautiously, he peeled his bare arms away from his quivering face. His eyes squinted at the powerful beams in front of him, forcing his head to turn away in an abrupt manner.

'Hey, hey! What the hell are you doing, mate... are you alright?' asked a deep voice from within the lights.

Daniel whimpered as the brightness stung his salty eyes; he focused his vision, straining as he peered through the gaps in his open hand. It was just a man in a car, he was safe. He collapsed onto the freezing tarmac and began to sob. His sanity was almost at breaking point. Suddenly, a high pitched sound—like static interference—drove through his skull. He clasped his head with both hands, desperate to keep out the horrific noise. His nose began to bleed heavily, running thickly down and over his dry, shrivelled lips. He scrambled to his numb feet, grimacing as the noise pierced his crumbling brain.

He looked to the Heavens, spinning in a complete circle as he scanned the sky. Amber and white lights pulsed silently from afar. A large, oval-shaped silhouette tilted as it began to carve its way through the darkness. His bloodshot eyes opened wide, and his mouth fell as he began to stutter.

'Are you okay, do you need an ambulance?' asked the young blonde-haired stranger again.

Daniel raised his shaking left arm and pointed to the sky. 'Can't you see it?' he asked as his finger fixated on the object. 'Look, there!' The tears began to race with the blood that trickled down his pale face. 'No, leave me alone!'

He twisted his body and began running. The extreme pain in his right hand made him contort violently with every awkward step that he took.

The owner of the car looked to the skies, bemused, before switching his focus back to this bizarre man. He watched as Daniel shrank to a tiny speck as he got farther away. He stood motionless with his hand on top of the car door. A slight vibration underneath his feet—and throughout the car—averted his attention momentarily. With a loud pop that sounded like a gunshot, all of the windows of the red Ford hatchback shattered. The stranger instinctively crouched in shock, protecting himself as cubes of glass showered down, bouncing off the tarmac.

The brightly lit shape hummed as it passed over the top of him. A seamless strip of amber lighting ran around the rim of the 100 metre long craft's base; the colour glowed in panelled sections underneath the dark shadow, its structure distorted by a wispy vapour. More amber lights—small and pitted—adorned its rim in a double circular row. With ease, it began chasing down the naked man.

The stranger stared in disbelief as the lights stopped 250 yards from where he stooped, unable to comprehend the situation. A luminous blue light emanated from the ship, shooting downwards like a lightning bolt as broken screams echoed in the distance. His green eyes looked around to see if anybody else was witnessing the events. He turned back to where the lights were, but they were gone—and so was the distant, naked figure.

Raucous sounds dominated the room. Daniel opened his eyes gingerly; his cloudy vision gradually started to clear. He gazed round, still in a stupor; he began to tremble as the surroundings became familiar.

The faint orange ceiling light gently tried to penetrate the reddish mist that hung heavily in the air. The smell of rotting flesh suddenly made him gag—it was atrocious. He became aware of the aching in his right hand which, he realised had now been poorly bandaged. The blood from the earlier nosebleed had dried and become matted to his dark stubble. Though the coppery odour that wafted uninvitingly up his nostrils was a welcome relief to the other smells around him.

The heaviness in his mind began to disintegrate as he remembered exactly where he was. In a swift effort he leapt forward, forgetting the pain as he grabbed the steel bars that stood solid before him. His worst fears were confirmed—he was back in one of the six-feet cubed cages that occupied the cargo hold of the alien ship.

'Let me out of here you fucking grey bastards!' he shouted.

Instantly, the cage rattled hard as two, long leathery-skinned hands gripped the bars above his own white knuckles. He knelt, frightened as the hands were followed by large black stoney eyes. A slit-like mouth flatlined across its oval face as a hot feeling began to intrude on his thoughts.

That's right human, that's why you were selected. Your hatred knows no bounds!

The words of the alien echoed around Daniel's thumping skull. He struggled to understand how the being spoke, especially since its mouth failed to move. He guessed that it was some form of telepathy, that was the only explanation. With that, the alien shook the cage again as though teasing a tied up pet. Daniel fell onto his backside, still unable to stop the shaking. He squirmed in the dirt, kicking out at the bizarre, grubby little insects that shared the confined space with him.

He couldn't think straight; his brain felt scrambled. Whimpers and cries emanated from the hundreds of cages that lined the cargo hold. He stretched as tall as possible, and stared across the vast space, at the perfectly positioned rows of steel. Each row had a two-foot drop below the long stretches of the wide metal walkways. It was like a giant warehouse. Startled, he jumped as four Greys walked across the level grating. He crawled back away from the bars. From the shadows he observed quietly, as the seven-feet tall skinny creatures dragged a huge purple mass out from the corridor. A brown vinegar-like substance trailed behind the smooth lump, followed by six extremely long tendrils with black claws attached to them. He struggled to contain his fear, watching as the tendrils snaked through the wet mess that puddled on the walkway as it passed.

A monstrous roar came from an identical cage opposite, 20 feet across the walkway. He moved even closer to the bars, his face pressed hard into them as he peered through the red tinge. A hulking, purple-skinned figure hunched under the roof of its prison. The same tendrils and black claws had wrapped themselves around the steel and were shaking the cube from side to side. Two golden reptilian eyes stared deep into his soul.

Daniel began laughing hysterically as the madness skipped hand in hand with his snapping sanity. 'You look like something out of Sesame Street!' he mocked, pointing to the outraged beast.

The aliens slid the purple mass into a dank corner of the cargo hold. Its bulk exhaled slightly as the low light cast a minimal shadow onto the wall. It was still alive, though barely. One of the Greys bent down and loomed over the body. Its slender four-fingered hands crawled spider-like over the torso, before engulfing the dying beast's massive head. With a hard twist, the alien completely removed the head from the thick muscular neck. Brown liquid spat outwards; the spurt slowed to a steady stream, blending into a single line that seeped down the dangling muscles. The Grey casually tossed the severed head onto the lifeless body.

Daniel gazed into the corpse's still open eyes. A lump rose in his already strained throat. He turned to the caged monster who wailed opposite him. 'I'm sorry,' he said as his grin had now disappeared. It didn't matter what planet you were from, death was still a loss—in any language.

The empty cage next to his began to automatically rise from its two-foot drop. It stopped with a loud clatter as it sat flush with the walk-way. A naked human man slid across the flooring as he was thrown in with force. The man was difficult to identify; he looked almost Nean-derthal in appearance with his long black hair and beard. The wild look in his blue eyes told their own story as he scrambled for cover behind the bars. He was strewn with blood that ran from the many wounds that covered his malnourished body. He began screaming hysterically as the cage door slammed shut. Daniel knew that the man's spirit was already broken as the cage began lowering back down into the drop.

'Who are you, how long have you been here?' asked Daniel as the cage hit the flooring. He was desperate for some form of companionship, some answers. 'Who are you?' There was silence. Finally he got a response as the crazed eyes connected with his own.

'Davidé ... mon nom est Davidé,' said the man as he pointed to Daniel's bandaged hand.

Daniel dropped his tired head in despair. *The only other human I have seen here and he's from France! He may as well be from another planet—I can't speak fucking French!*

Davidé sat in the dirt, rocking back and forth. He looked at Daniel before crying maniacally. Daniel was becoming frustrated with the Frenchman. He pushed the side of his face back up against the bars, as though trying to squeeze his head through them.

'Why did they hurt my hand, but make such an effort to keep me?' he said as his skin pressed against the steel. 'DO—YOU—UNDERSTAND—ME?'

Davidé stared blankly as the tears fell from his worn face; his soul just wasn't there anymore.

Daniel sighed, discouraged. It was like trying to make a small child understand him. He placed his mouth through the gap in between the bars. 'GOD DAMN YOU, LET ME OUT!' he raged as his hands rattled the cage violently.

He could feel the absurdity at his actions as the pain soared. The disruption caused many of the other captives to become as enraged as he was. It sounded like a chaotic zoo as the shouts and cries spread across the air. He attempted to calm himself, watching as a blue scaly arm protruded from another cage. Staring right, across the opposite line, he followed the rough fingers that caused the mist to trail off in broken circles as they felt for freedom.

Glancing upwards, he could see the Greys walking up and down the metal walkways. Through the tinge he could see their feet, right up to their waists as they walked from row to row, acting as security, observing the madness. He imagined their large heads hovering above the haze, and the menacing stare that came from those empty black eyes. He thought of how scared he was each time they strode past his cage, wondering if they were coming for him. He shivered at the mental images.

The blue three-fingered hand grabbed at one of the Greys as it passed. The alien stooped and looked down at the flailing limb, death emanating from its every fibre. It produced a short silver pencil-like device; its finger stretched over the line of tiny buttons that ran down the gadget's shiny surface. A luminous green laser shot out from the end of the thin metallic object. Daniel watched in horror as the light stream sliced the appendage clean off, like a knife through butter. A mustard-coloured liquid poured from the wound, dropping in heavy lumps onto the walkway. The creature let out a mighty wail that shot around the slimy walls. Daniel immediately released his grip from the bars, and quietly returned to the corner of his prison.

'Shut up! Shut up!' he shouted as he placed his trembling hands over his ears. The animalistic noises had begun to take their toll. The cage juddered as it began to rise from its drop. He closed his eyes tight and began to sing aloud: 'God save our gracious Queen, long live our noble Queen—'

His arms dropped slowly from his head as he opened his eyes, terrified. One of the grey creatures was bent down, staring straight at him. The alien cocked its curious head to one side. Daniel could see that it was flanked either side by two more of its comrades. It waved its hand in a nonchalant, dismissive manner. A dark grey miniature triangle—the size of a 20 pence piece—glowed with red lines. Twang! The sharp sound of unlocking steel shook his senses. The cage door sprung open with a jolt from its DNA-operated lock. The creature stepped back, allowing the two others to step inside the cage. They crouched down as they crawled into the filthy, claustrophobic space, giving Daniel no room to manoeuvre.

'No, no, no, no!' he cried, shuffling backwards until his body met with the cold hard bars. He tried kicking at the outstretched gangly limbs thrusting towards him. It was futile as a tight pressure gripped both his arms and ankles. 'What are you doing to me, I demand to know what you are doing to me!' He screamed out as their hands clamped around his bones. They began to drag him through the dirt, and out of his prison.

The two aliens held Daniel by each wrist. They pulled him viciously through the bodily fluids that were covering the walkway grating. His bare heels slid through the trailing innards that came from across the universe. As he lay on his back, gliding through the grim mess, he stared at the steel prisons that he passed. One after the other, a different bizarre creature from some distant world looked back at him. They, like himself, were prisoners of whatever this was. Some sat quietly, gazing emptily into the air. Others spoke strange languages as they tried to reason with their abductors. He even heard other human voices begging for their freedom. Some lay wounded, moaning loudly, their pain unbearable. Most lay dead, heaps of limbs and putrid rotting flesh.

A continuous line of blurred orange light and uninterrupted steel passed overhead until the Greys stopped. Daniel flopped his sweaty head backwards, watching as the extraterrestrial flicked its hand across the larger, yet otherwise identical triangular sensor. A solid grey door screeched open with speed. The area that they entered was deathly quiet. There was no mist as the white light illuminated the hexagonal-shaped room. He looked from left to right, panicking as he was lifted onto an extremely long rectangular table. He inhaled sharply as the cold, metallic surface touched his bare flesh. The sensation sent the hairs on his body into shivery overdrive.

The room had a sterilised smell—an almost bleach-like quality about it. He squinted hard at the white light overhead; it hung like a piece of string, slowly lowering itself with a mechanical whirring. He tried to move his arms to protect his face from the hot glow, but he couldn't—he was paralysed.

He began breathing erratically. The three creatures moved back from the table as a series of holes opened within its surface. A fourth being bent over him and looked directly into his eyes. The monotone voice that followed, spiked his brain... This is going to hurt.

Moist fingers grasped Daniel's sweaty head, turning it with a sadistic purpose to the right. A trail of saliva trickled from the corner of his half open mouth, and dribbled down his white cheek. His chest felt like it was going to explode as he watched the lead alien cruelly rip the soiled bandages from his wounded hand. The smell that greeted him made his face contort in disgust. He managed to raise his head and stare at his hand. Lumps of yellow pus had thickened around his fingers, sticking them together. His raw hand thumped with an excruciating stinging pain. His heart sank; he knew that his hand was badly infected.

Two instruments—similar to the pencil devices, but larger—were held aloft. Loud piercing sounds shot from the vibrating tools, followed by red glows. The alien looked at Daniel again. This time we will hurt you properly! The words bounced around his head like a thousand rubber balls as the lasers went to work, drilling through the non-anaesthetised limb; the stench of burning flesh overpowered the air amidst a downpour of sparks.

Daniel's agonised scream reverberated through the corridor, beating the walls like invisible fists as the lasers entered his bones. His body jerked with each deeper penetration. A blackness descended around the room; it shrouded the aliens, blurring their heads into fuzzy silhouettes. His nose began to bleed again, joining the saliva in a gooey thickness. His eyes rolled backwards into his head as his body started to convulse. He passed out from the pain...

He awoke to the familiar sounds of animalistic howls, his return to consciousness welcomed by the vile smell of death. His blurred eyes slowly travelled the large "zoo". He flinched at the intense pain caused by the hefty weight that was his right hand. With his left, he clawed at the grease and grime as he tried to shift his bare body into an upright position. His sweat-ravaged forehead hurt badly from the brightness of the hexagonal room; the black spots in his vision caused him to shake his head, enhancing the excruciating pain. Digging his heels into the oily floor, he managed to place his back against cool steel. He was back in the cage.

He looked left at the cage next to his—Davidé was gone. He writhed painfully until he was on his knees, scanning the room through the bars as he tried to gain some insight into what was happening, and why. His eyes searched every inch as far as they could go, but the visibility still wasn't good as the red mist surrounded the area.

The pain didn't decrease. This was coupled with tremendous hunger. With all this happening he realised that he hadn't drunk, or eaten anything since his arrival. Somehow though, he desperately needed to empty his bowels. Despite everything that he had seen, and what he was going through, he felt embarrassed about having to defecate so openly.

Primal urge took place of pride as he crawled to the back of the cage. He held his shaking right hand tight to his chest, and straightened his upper body. Remaining on his knees, he parted his legs slightly. He emptied his bowels, moaning in discomfort at the effort. The foreign insects immediately began to investigate as the watery contents congealed on the dirty surface.

With half closed eyes he looked around sheepishly, before placing his left hand under his shrivelled penis. He proceeded to urinate into and over the palm, spilling it as he tried to steady his arm. Quickly, he raised his grubby hand to his dry mouth and began slurping at the warm, dark orange urine. He started gagging violently at the disgusting taste, but he knew that he needed it. The urine that he managed to keep down eased his sore throat until he gagged again. His left hand fell to the floor; the drips entwined with his fingers. He closed his tired eyes and dropped his head in shame; even now, he tried to maintain some dignity. Those who watched probably did not know what he was doing, or even care. Deep down though, he understood that this little embarrassment might prolong his life longer.

He stared at the inch-long bugs as they gathered around the faeces, amused by their long legs struggling to negotiate the congealing, sticky pool. Something flashed which caught his eye. He moved slowly on his hand and knees towards the puddle of defecation, wincing with each movement. He studied the contents closely, then dipped his left thumb and index finger awkwardly into the muck. He delicately pulled out a small hard object. He spat onto his thumb, and rubbed the flat quarter-inch metallic square between his fingers. He spat a second time before finally wiping his hand against his icy left thigh. He raised the object to his eye-line, staring intensely as he tried to work out what it was. A tiny yellow light pulsed from the maze of minuscule, vine-like circuitry that branched out over the object.

'What the fuck?' He rotated the metal between his fingers, letting out a sigh. He knew what it was. He opened his mouth—splitting his dry lips in the process—and placed the gadget between his uneven teeth, biting hard. A bitter taste forced him to spit out the bent, damaged square. The light was dead, the circuitry mangled. A curl lipped scowl dominated his dirty features. 'Fucking tracking devices.'

A fever was beginning to take hold—even in the cold atmosphere, the sweat poured from his head. Screams continued to puncture his senses as his head and hand burned heavily. He tried to raise his right hand, but the effort was too much. The sound of footsteps on the grating soon forced him to hunch back in the weak light. He began to shake as the three aliens returned. Their thin bodies cast long shadows as they passed by his cage. He let out a relieved breath, pursing his lips as he balanced his fragility out evenly with the little sanity that remained.

The creatures were dragging another bloodied body, except this one had no head. An arm fell from the corpse, swaying hypnotically from side to side like a gruesome pendulum. Filth and germs congregated under broken nails in small clumps as the fingers scraped the bacteria-infested flooring.

Daniel groaned gently to himself as he recognised that the arm was human. His tear-glazed eyes followed the body, watching as it was dumped ruthlessly into the corner amongst the otherworldly corpses; it was like a universal mass morgue as the bodies began to pile up. One of the Greys held the human head by its tangled web of dark hair. The alien's eyes—black, emotionless—exuded nothing as the head was thrown onto the death pile. Daniel inhaled as his heart skipped a beat. The head landed with a sickening thud. Blue eyes stared back at him in frozen terror—it was Davidé.

Daniel opened his eyes abruptly, blinking repetitively as he tried to focus. He lay half upright in the dirt. I must have passed out again he thought as the screams burrowed once again into his shattered brain. The smell snaked up his nose, causing him to clench his eyes shut for a few seconds. He jumped, feeling the insects crawling over his naked body; their harsh legs scratched irritatingly at his flesh. He attempted to bat them off as he hoisted himself up fully. Sighing nervously, he stared at the floor; he couldn't tell if it was steel or not as there was so much muck covering it.

The cage shuddered again as it slowly rose, culminating in a strong jolt. The murky shadows forced his stare from the floor. His dazed face looked up at the three figures squatting at the front bars of the cage. Their forms blurred back and forth as he struggled to maintain focus. He felt an acidic burn as bile entered his throat. The alien waved its hand through the air and the steel door flew open. Again, the creature stood back as the other two entered the cage, grabbing at him. He tried to fight their advances, but was too weak; it was useless—they overpowered him effortlessly.

He gazed at the wavering, fading orange light as he was pulled roughly down the corridor. This time he was being was taken a different way, as his body shifted around several corners and along as many corridors. Apart from the light, all he could see was the back of the aliens' long necks. He stared uneasily at the small rolls of rumpled skin that stretched out with each giant step. His ears pricked as he heard violent growls mixed with shrieking cries. They stopped at another door. He leant his delirious head back as the Grey moved its hand across the sensor. The large door opened slowly; it didn't seem as efficient as the others, somewhat at a technical disadvantage. More low level light greeted him as they entered the large circular room. Another corpse, this time brown and hairy, passed by him. There was no mist as he strained his neck sideways, watching as the leathery hands dragged the thing out of the door.

They all stopped. The aliens pulled Daniel to his feet with force. A fiery pain made him nauseous as his head hung to one side, his body semi-conscious and shivering. The leader of the three Greys descended before him. Time to die! He could feel its deep eyes burn his soul as his brain absorbed its grim words.

He looked around the room, unsure of where he was. A 40-foot dull grey metal pit swallowed them all up. Several feet in front of him was a bright blue electrical forcefield. He had no idea what it was for, and tried to gape through its sparse transparency.

Many Greys, hundreds, gathered on the upper steps of the steel coliseum. They looked on as the bandages were ripped from Daniel's right hand. It was like a cattle market as the Greys all looked to one another, pointing in communication to where he stood. He flinched as the last portion of bandage was brutally torn away, causing him to collapse. The aliens lifted him back to his feet, but the sight of his hand almost made him pass out again. There, mechanically and surgically fused to his right hand, was a rusted four-pronged fork-like weapon. He stared in a dream-like state at the horrific appendage that was once his healthy human hand. He felt dizzy, unsteady on his feet as he rotated his wrist; blood swam with the rust, and ever increasing infection.

The Greys surrounding him removed themselves from the 12 foot deep pit and joined their fellow species in the stands. Daniel raised his flittering eyes to the shadowy forms that stood the other side of the strange forcefield. Narrowing his eyes, he could vaguely make out another three stick thin figures.

A loud buzzer sounded, startling him. The blue forcefield wall disappeared with a static crackle. He watched as the aliens in front of his eye-line parted, and proceeded to climb out of the pit. The thing that looked back at him scared him to the brink of vomiting.

He looked around the eerily quiet room. His eyes trawled the crowd's faces, empty, still. The buzzer sounded again, making him jump once more. He turned his slow attention back to the pit which made him smile insanely. It reminded him of an empty swimming pool, though why he found this amusing he didn't know.

The tall green creature sprinted forwards athletically on its two kangaroo-like legs. Its jagged distorted figure danced in spasms as it headed towards him. As it came nearer, Daniel could see that it also had a similar type of weapon fused to its muscular right arm.

The strange monster swung its blades as it attempted to kill him. His maniacal face—swamped in terror—watched as the creature's moist skin sparkled in the glow. He panicked, instinctively ducking and diving as the foggy onslaught continued. Two small red eyes glowed as they hunted their prey; rows of sharp teeth dripped thick saliva as they craved his flesh, his death.

He staggered around the pit in an adrenaline-induced motion—there was nowhere to hide. The faces blended into a grey swirl within the crowd as he sought safety. He looked for a way out, at the singular steps that jutted out from the side of the pit. But it was no good, he was too weak to haul himself out anyway.

The creature blocked his every move, cutting him off in all directions. He swung blindly at it, desperate to escape. He threw his weak arm out in a pushing, prodding motion. It roared as he caught it in the midriff with his weaponised hand; chunks of green wrinkled flesh dangled from the dirty blades. It took a big step backwards, stunned at the sight of the four deep slash wounds that lined its thick flesh. The scowl deepened as it composed itself, grinding its teeth angrily before leaping forwards.

Instinct took hold as Daniel's cloudy vision cleared slightly, making him more aware. Sadly this was not to last. In one swift movement, four long claws gripped his wiry right arm. The creature raised its steel pincer towards the human's struggling wrist. With a scissor snip, it cut. Clang! The sound reverberated around the arena as the weapon—and what was left of Daniel's hand—fell to the floor. He let out a blood curdling scream that became an assault on the alien crowds' senses. The burning sensation climbed his arm, shredding his nerve endings in searing, blistering agony.

The extraterrestrial watchers seemed agitated. Whether this was their way of showing excitement or not, Daniel didn't know, nor care. The creature moved its clawed hand from his arm, creeping it up to his neck. He was trapped like a fly in a spider web. He threw his left arm wildly in a desperate arc as the creature's claws entered his soft pale flesh. A large, horned face thrust itself into his eye-line. He could feel its hot vulgar breath as it blasted his worn, sweat-laden skin. He began to cry as his sanity finally cracked. The monster seemed taken aback at the human's streaking tears; it seemed as though it had never encountered such behaviour until now. Daniel raised his left arm as he tried to fight off the choking hold from his withering neck. The attempts were always futile, he knew this, he just didn't have the energy—or the will—to survive anymore.

The creature's face was covered in tiny, pointed lumps. These seemed to diminish, soften, as it began sniffing curiously at the bloodied stump that was once Daniel's right hand. It raised its weapon and began jabbing at the fragile body in front of it. Daniel wailed at each vicious prod as lumps of flesh were torn from his weak torso. Stinging torment arrived on the deep wounds that were dotted randomly over his skin. Flashes of rib bones glistened with blood in the light. The creature snorted as it seemed to momentarily study his human anatomy, picking at the holes as it peered into the wounds.

'Please... please... let me go,' whispered Daniel as his tear-stained red eyes roamed the arena. He let out a high pitched whine which stunned the creature back into its fighting posture. It tightened its hold around his neck. Its eyes came alive, glowing as the aggression spread over its grotesque face. Daniel heard—and felt a swift cracking sound. He was finding it hard to breathe as he began to waver. His eyes blurred once more as they lost focus. The crowd seemed to sway hypnotically, side to side as they took on a slow, bendy appearance. He could hear his heartbeat pulsing in his head, petering by the second. The darkness quickly followed...

The flaccid body hung heavily as it was dragged through to the freezing cargo hold. A never-ending chorus of cries and wails dominated the oppressive air.

'Help me! Help!' begged a human female voice that quickly faded from within reach of passing alien ears.

The Grey that followed banged on the side of a cage. This silenced the growling coming from behind the bars. The three humanoids stopped in their smooth tracks and lifted the body up. In one effort it landed on the death pile with a wet, heavy slap. It was followed by bunched up metres of slimy, unravelled intestines—and Daniel's badly severed head. His dark eyes, dead... nothing.

Chapter 3

Unrest

'Monsters, they're all fucking monsters!' said Mark, his usually calm demeanour rattled as he made frantic hand gestures.

'What the hell had they done to him?' asked James, as he sat with his head between his knees. 'W-w-why was he in pieces?'

Hargreaves puffed out his red cheeks. 'Must have been some form of experimentation,' he said, trying to remain composed, 'either that or torture, take your pick.'

'But what sort of torturer does that to a person?' James said, raising his head to look at them. 'Are we next, do you think?'

Tom had begun to squirm in the grease on the floor; he was at breaking point. The others all just stared at him; they had given up, there was no calming him anymore.

'Well, we know that we can't get off this ship now, especially after what I've just witnessed,' said Mark with a nervous sigh as the full realisation sunk deep. 'We aren't going anywhere.'

John had also started to become agitated as he raised his voice to speak over Tom's incessant noise. 'What do we do, wait for them to come in and take us one by one?'

Mark began to pace the perimeter of the wall. 'We don't know what's going to happen.'

'Come on, Mark, don't bullshit around,' said John, 'we're all dead, aren't we?' The writhing and wailing within the room had reached an intolerable level. The noise burrowed through John's skull, driving like a corkscrew through his brain. He placed his hands over his ears. 'Will you stop fucking shouting, I can't think straight!'

'Calm down, all of you,' reasoned Mark as he moved towards John. He raised his hands chest high, so his motions could be seen through the mist.

John clenched his fists. 'I'll calm down when he shuts up!'

Tom lay on the floor with a crazed look upon his face. He pointed a dirty finger at John. 'Dead, dead, dead!'

'No, don't do it.' Mark could see what was coming. He tried to hold onto John's left arm, but his feet began slipping from underneath him. 'General, some help please.'

John ran over to Tom and began kicking him while he spun on the grating, laughing and crying simultaneously.

'Stop it!' screamed James as he fell on top of Tom to protect him. 'He doesn't know what he's saying.'

Tom clung to James's slender frame like a frightened child as Hargreaves approached John from behind. He hooked his arms underneath the attacker's medium build as he tried in vain to apply a full nelson hold. He struggled to get the right grip through the thick material of his military blazer, though the younger man's strength didn't help matters. Finally, Hargreaves managed to interlock his fingers at the back of John's fleshy neck. They both slid backwards into the wall as John swung his body in a circle, kicking out as he attempted to break the hold. His power eventually gave in as he tired out. The General may have been double in John's age, but he was equal in strength when it came down to it.

'Fucking let me go,' panted John as his arms went loose by his shoulders. 'I'm done, alright.'

Hargreaves' large barrel-shaped chest rose and fell rhythmically as he regained his breath. 'Are you sure?' he said firmly.

John patted the General's forearms. 'Yeah, I'm done.'

Hargreaves cautiously released his grip and pushed the man forwards, away from him. John staggered off, rubbing the back of his neck.

'Right, General, what would the military do in a situation such as this?' asked Mark now that the conflict had settled.

'First things first: remain calm and survey your surroundings. Once the option of any escape routes has been removed, then prepare for interrogation—and possible torture.'

The General's words stung their ears.

'But why would they interrogate us, and for what purpose?' James said as he held Tom to keep him warm. 'Surely, they know everything anyway, don't they?'

'No,' said Hargreaves in a deep tone as he walked towards the others. 'They never know everything.'

John was now calm, though the back of his neck still felt sore as he crouched down against the wall. 'Help us out here, General… What's the military up to?'

'Forget all of your questions, the General can't tell you,' whispered Mark. 'This might be the whole point of us being here, do you understand?'

'What do you mean?'

'Look, this could all be an alien exercise in an attempt to gain military knowledge. For all we know we could have been handpicked specifically, in terms of our personalities.'

James looked up at the Professor. 'I don't follow,' he said with a frown, 'what have our personalities got to do with anything?'

Hargreaves moved into the middle of the group, nodding in agreement with the Professor. 'Well, they might have placed Tom here purposefully because of his mental state—knowing that he would crack, knowing that one of us wouldn't be able to handle the noise, for example. Maybe Mark is here for his rational thought, or more likely his extensive scientific education. Perhaps they know that James' nature would side with Tom, I could go on…'

John and James slowly looked around the room as though the creatures were watching and listening. Tom was becoming restless again; James gently stroked his sweaty brow to ease the man's fears.

'All I will say—AND THAT GOES OUT TO THE ALIEN BASTARDS THAT ARE LISTENING—is that the military will never give up, so long as there's fight left in them!'

John raised an eyebrow. 'I hope you're right, General, I hope you're right.'

Mark placed a soft hand upon John's shoulder. 'They are probably out there now, engaging the enemy to protect us all. Hell, we could even be winning!' he said, determined to strengthen the mood. He then looked to the General. 'Could be why we're here, so they can gather the information from us that they need, you know, because they are losing?!'

'That is quite possible, Professor, I wouldn't put anything past these bastards,' said Hargreaves, rubbing his hands together in an effort to keep warm.

James pulled himself away from Tom; he let the body slide carefully out of his arms as he cradled Tom's head, protecting it from hitting the floor. He placed his own rough hand over Tom's mouth, trying to stifle the oncoming fear. The trembling response jarred the grating hard. Everyone looked to him as they feared the worst.

Hargreaves rolled his eyes as Tom's whining finally shattered his calm thoughts. 'Will you shut up, Tom!' he snapped. He turned and straightened his uniform again.

'General, take it easy,' said Mark with a firm glare, trying to keep everyone level headed.

'Don't tell me to "take it easy". Who the hell do you think you are?'

Mark was taken aback by the sharp tone. 'General, I know that you're angry, we all are, but this isn't helping.'

Hargreaves turned and faced Mark. 'Isn't helping?' he laughed. 'You would know all about helping, wouldn't you!'

'What are you going on about, General, what are you trying to say?' Mark's cool exterior was also beginning to deteriorate. 'Don't skirt the issue, if you've got something to say, say it.'

Hargreaves' eyes narrowed as he came face to face with the Professor. 'You really have no idea, no inkling of what you did—found?'

Mark shook his head in confusion. 'No, General, I don't.'

The others began to take interest in the heated conversation; their curious eyes and ears concentrated on the unfolding scene before them.

Hargreaves noticed. He watched their expressions through the thin veil of mist. 'Don't any of you remember the Californian blackout, the day that history was changed forever? Ah, no, you wouldn't know because it was quickly covered up. But let me tell you all about our good Professor here.' Hargreaves almost revelled in his oneupmanship over Mark as he turned his attention back to the Professor. 'Our man here is part of a genius group at Stanford, a group which successfully discovered time travel!'

'Time travel?' said John with a quizzical look.

'Yes, though they only managed to go one way—backwards.' Hargreaves moved closer to Mark, his body language becoming aggressive. 'Tell them what little fragments remain, Professor. Tell them what you found.'

Mark felt fear as all stares centred on him. Even though the room was dim, their eyes seemed to burn through his skin. 'I don't know, it's all pieces,' he said.

'I don't wish to crush anyone, but tell them,' said Hargreaves as he poked the Professor's chest with his index finger. 'Tell them the truth, or I will!'

'I CAN'T REMEMBER ANYTHING!' shouted Mark as the paranoia took hold. He paused for a few seconds before continuing 'If it's that bad, General, then why do you seem intent on destroying these people? I mean, what's your incentive, eh, why do you want to disrupt us further, what's in it for you?'

The others now looked at Hargreaves with an instant distrust. He quickly combed his silver hair with his hand, a gesture which signalled his discomfort.

John rose from his squatted position, and adjusted his clothing. 'General?'

'Don't you dare turn this on me! I'm looking out for you all,' answered Hargreaves angrily, his ageing facial skin turning crimson. 'Without me you won't stand a chance!'

'Yeah,' James said as he let out a breath, 'again, look what happened to Daniel.'

'Okay, enough is enough!' said John suddenly as he walked between the two bickering experts. 'Look, we're all in this together, right? None of us are going anywhere if you two keep arguing.' He continued to look from one to the other. 'General, you knew about the invasion. It's okay, that's old news. Mark, whatever you know, well, forget it. It's all about the now, and what the fuck are we going to do about it!'

The two professionals looked to each other, embarrassed by their childish behaviour. John was right, it was all about the current situation.

'I'm sorry, General, I didn't mean anything in what I said. We're all frazzled by this, but you have to understand, I'm no different to the rest of you,' Mark said with sincerity.

Hargreaves cleared his throat. 'Yes, er, I know.'

Mark scratched his head. He smiled as he knew that the General was not a man to openly apologise, he was too proud for that. He nodded to him anyway, to which a large hand sprung outwards in his direction. The men shook hands firmly—this was the apology, and Mark was more than happy to accept it at this point.

'My God, we've been here for all this time,' said Hargreaves, visibly tired. 'The world, I wonder what state the world is really in?' He looked to the floor. 'Is this it, the end of life… is it over?'

Mark let his body slide down against the wall. He was just as tired as he dropped his head in his hands.

'I think it is, General—it's the end of days.'

The minutes ticked by in silence.

Hargreaves looked up at the others; he realised that the mood wasn't good. 'Listen up. I know that this is an inappropriate time, but there is possibly some good news,' he whispered as events played over in his mind.

'Good news?' replied James as he lifted his blue gaze towards the General. 'What news could you have that would possibly be good?'

A flicker of hope glowed across Hargreaves' line-filled face as he dismissed the sarcasm. 'Think about it. In situations such as these, no matter in what periods of humanity, there have always been groups, resistance. These have carried on the war during the threat of annihilation.'

'Yes, General. As much as I agree with you, this all depends on how many of the population remain,' said Mark. 'Don't forget, the human race has never dealt with a threat such as this, well, except for viruses like the Black Death maybe.'

'Oh, Professor, I'm surprised at your defeatist attitude.' Hargreaves shook his head. 'Look at the wars of the past; how many times has a rebellion overcome invasion with limited numbers and less advanced weaponry?' They all listened intently as the General hit his stride. 'The Battle of Thermopylae, where the vastly outnumbered allied Greeks held off Xerxes' Persian army for seven days... seven days!'

Mark smiled at the history lesson. 'With all due respect, General, this is different. Xerxes' army wasn't as huge as was thought. Don't get me wrong, it was 150,000 strong at most, but this isn't a swords and spears war.'

'Professor, you're missing the point. The point is that they managed to survive the impossible for a short time. Let's just say that the military never puts all their eggs in one basket, that's one thing that history has taught us.'

'And remind us all of the outcomes, General?' interrupted James. 'The fact that they all lost in the end, died?'

'Enough of the bloody history lessons!' said John, cutting their flow. The two men turned their attention back to one another.

'What are you trying to say, General?' asked Mark as he narrowed his dark eyes, ignoring John's comments.

Hargreaves looked around at the dull walls, cautious as to who—or what—may be listening, before he realised he had said too much.

Yeah, I understand. Mark gave a nod in Hargreaves' direction.

'Besides, if the worst comes to the worst we have other weapons that could be used,' said Hargreaves with a wry smile.

'Brilliant! More hidden weapons,' said James as he threw his arms up. 'Let me guess, chemical? Tested on an unsuspecting village somewhere in the Middle East?'

Mark looked at Hargreaves.

'Don't be so naïve, Professor. This is why such things are created; we need protection against scenarios such as these we face now. I don't think the survivors would care too much, so long as the current threat was eliminated, do you?'

Mark had to concede defeat. He wasn't in total agreement concerning the military's potential course of action, but the General was right once again. 'Okay, so if chemicals work, then what state would the lands be left in? How would humanity survive when it comes to growing food for example, surely the land would be contaminated?'

'I think that the survivors would have more than enough land to cope with,' said Hargreaves. 'We need to keep fighting back otherwise the human race will become extinct!'

'Then the only hope is to hide and breed, don't you think?'

Hargreaves shook his head. 'Mark, the longer these invaders are here, the harder it will become to beat them. It won't be too long before they break down our best weapons; they will deconstruct them, analyse them, destroy them. It's standard military procedure, you find out the enemy's weaknesses, which in this case here happens to be us.'

'How can we be the weakness here? I don't get it,' said James with a scowl.

Hargreaves turned to the youngster. 'Because neither of us wants to be next, let alone the last one left. You wound the mind, get it to think that one can be saved if—'

'If you give them the information they want,' said Mark, finishing off the General's sentence. 'It's the same as Daniel. They opened that door to show us because they wanted to, not because they had to. After all, by doing it to you, General, it would have been pointless. They know that such threats would be useless against you as you've been trained for this type of scenario. They did it for fun.'

'This is my point, Professor, you wound the mind.'

'Oh, I understand, General, I do. But these aren't 2000 year old Romans, Greeks, or whoever that we are dealing with. This is an invasion, if in fact that is what is happening now. Furthermore, we still don't know where we are; we are on a ship, yes, but is it one, or one of many? Are we still in the Earth's atmosphere, or far away from it?

'At the end of the day—and there may not be many of them left—whether they are Roman, Greek, or extraterrestrial, it doesn't matter.'

'How so,' asked Mark, intrigued.

'Because an enemy is still an enemy. They still have one and the same goals, and those are to occupy, conquer and colonise.'

The steam from John's urine rose amongst the haze. The smell had become stronger, as this particular corner of the room was where all of the waste now congregated. He finished and returned to the group. Tom's head lay on James' left shoulder, watching as Mark picked at a strange insect that had wandered into view. The General balanced his weight as he squatted against the wall. They all remained in silence. Without warning, the panel began to glow. The exhausted bodies bolted upright, alert as they prepared themselves for what was coming next.

Tom began trembling as the door shot open. A fearful whine left his thirsty mouth as he focused on the shadows through the mist. Hands clasped each other as two of the aliens entered the room and approached James. The group leapt up and parted, scrambling aside as the shadowy forms moved in a staggered formation before lunging for his static body.

'Get off, get off!' he screamed, shaking his head sideways in child-like fear. They gripped his ankles, and with a hefty tug he fell to the floor; the metallic crash echoed around the room. 'Help me!' A ter-rifying aggression morphed over their smooth faces, wrinkling them briefly as they began to pull him across the floor. He tried to kick out, but his little strength had no effect on the wiry humanoids.

Tom fell back to the grating, whimpering as he placed his hands over his ears. He started pounding the sides of his head with his palms, in-creasing the voracity with each strike. His voice reached a high pitched tone as he shook his head from side to side. Suddenly, his timbre ran into a deep, angry cry. He climbed to his feet and ran at the beings, clawing at them like an angry beast as he sought to protect the man who had taken care of him.

He punched and scratched as he tried to loosen the aliens' grip. The Greys stopped, as though on pause for a few seconds before they turned their attention towards him. He now ceased his actions and began backing up against the wall. Another Grey pierced the haze as it entered the room. It turned and stood guard, warding off the adrenalin—pumped humans who jerked closer as they tried to inter-vene.

The creatures released their hold on James. Tom cried as one of the alien's struck him hard across the face, forcing him to the floor. They now grasped his left ankle and proceeded to drag him across the grating. He could see the silhouettes in the redness as his eyes strained wide. The shadows of the group became smaller—distant—as their cries fell to soft, frightened whispers.

'Tom!' shouted James as he clutched at the air from his position on the floor.

Monstrous roars filled the corridor. Tom looked back, his features frozen with fear as he desperately fumbled, scraping at the floor to gain some, any leverage. The noise outside faded within the room as he was pulled through the sliding doorway that closed rapidly.

'Why are they taking him?' asked James with a panicked expression on his face as he looked to Mark. 'He doesn't know anything, he's of no use to them.'

'Because they can,' said Hargreaves as he stood bent over with his hands on his knees.

Tom was gone and he wasn't coming back.

Chapter 4

Judgement Day—Tom's Story

The black rectangle buzzed on the oak bedside table as a brain-skewering melody played. Tom Valentine didn't know what was worse: the piercing ringtone that his wife, Connie, had secretly set on his phone, or the seemingly thunderous vibrations that shook him from his deep slumber. He craned his neck, watching as Connie stirred. He desperately wanted to avoid waking her as he knew that she would be grumpy come morning. He flung his right arm in an arc, and gently pushed down on the green telephone icon that flashed spritely in the dark. There was complete silence for several seconds as he hoisted himself upright. Yawning, he ruffled his ear length black hair with his left hand. Flicking the switch on the paisley patterned bedside lamp, he picked up the phone.

'Hello?'

'Tom? Tom, what the hell are you doing? Have you seen the—' replied the voice with urgency before being cut mid flow.

'What?' Tom asked, still half asleep as he strained his dark, sleep-filled eyes on the alarm clock. 'Who is this?'

'Wake up! Tom, it's me, Vincent.'

'Vincent? What are you doing, it's—' Tom looked at the clock as the digits glowed back at him in orange neon. 'It's 9:53 p.m. What's going on?'

Tom delicately pulled the deep blue duvet up and over Connie's bare porcelain-skinned shoulders. He smiled drowsily as her shock of curly red hair sprouted out from beneath the cover. He rubbed his eyes and winced as Vincent's voice boomed out from the tiny speaker.

'Shhh! Not so loud, you know I'll cop it tomorrow otherwise,' said Tom.

'9.53?' cackled Vincent, 'that's a bit early to be in bed, eh?'

'We've both got really early starts, so hurry up, I want to get back to sleep.'

'Anyway, forget that mate, you know I love Connie, but are you watching the news?'

'Of course I'm not. Like I said it's nine, well, 9:55 p.m. now.'

'Yeah, yeah, whatever,' said Vincent in a dismissive tone. 'PUT ON THE NEWS!'

Tom looked to Connie once more. With raised eyebrows he slowly and quietly slid out from the left side of the bed, shivering as he tip-toed across the plush aqua-green carpet. A contented sigh left his dry mouth as the soft material massaged the soles of his bare feet. He adjusted his boxer shorts, twisting them around until they were comfy. He crept over towards the television set that sat upon the oak drawers. He carefully picked up the remote control and gently pressed the ON button. He stared at his wife, still with the phone at his ear. The picture seeped onto the 32 inch screen in a series of fuzzy lines, finally settling as he selected the Sky News channel. What greeted his bleary eyes, jolted his system fully awake.

'Oh fuck, what the hell is that!' he said aloud as he sat hunched on the edge of the bed. He cringed as the bedsprings twanged, watching with a nervous tension as Connie rolled over. 'Shit!' He turned back to the TV set.

There, on screen, was the President of the United States of America. He stood in front of the White House insignia that emblazoned the blue velvet curtains in the press briefing room of the West Wing. The camera flashes dazzled all at this emergency meeting. Every journalist of importance congregated in hushed whispers as they tried to guess why they were there. The President's tall, slim build danced with slight agitation as he waited for the thumbs up to tell him start. To the top left of the screen was a set of images that were being repeatedly played over.

Tom sat stunned, wide-eyed as he drank in the video clips that were being sent in from all over the world.

The President's firm words commanded the journalistic audience from behind a crested hardwood podium. He stared down the lens of the TV camera as he addressed the world.

'Ladies and Gentlemen, members of the press, and the people of the world. Today, one of the most coveted questions in our history has been answered. No, we are not alone in the universe. Around one hour ago numerous unidentified craft entered our atmosphere, and proceeded to position themselves over many of the capital cities of the globe. As you can see from the footage that is pouring in, ships are still entering our air space as we speak.'

'At this moment in time we can't say why they are here, but we are working on several attempts at communicating with the vessels. I ask all citizens—not just of the USA but also of the planet—to remain calm. There will be many designated buildings open for help regarding questions, safety, and counselling if needed. Again, we don't know too much yet, so please be patient. There will be further updates as soon as more information is available.'

The President shuffled the crisp papers of his hastily written speech. He buttoned his navy blue pin-striped suit jacket before directing his firm gaze towards an astonished media.

'Mr. President, Karen Connors of the Seattle Times. How long have you known about their existence, I mean this can't be the first that you have heard of this?'

Connors leant forward in her red pencil thin skirt as she awaited the answer amidst a cacophony of voices.

The President looked directly into her blue eyes as he spoke. 'Hi, Miss Connors. 24 hours ago NASA informed me that the Hubble Space Telescope detected some strange emissions that, upon closer inspection, were deemed to be worthy of serious investigation. The astronauts on the International Space Station also reported that there were many short periods of intense static, along with some electrical shortages within their equipment caused by something of unknown origin.'

Connors' blonde hair bounced as she tilted her head, straining to hear. The constant mumblings in the room foiled her efforts.

'Settle down, please,' requested the President's aide as the panicked voices grew.

There was silence in the bedroom as the TV screen flickered with the camera flashes, lighting the walls around the bed.

'Fucking hell!' Tom said. 'Vincent, I'll call you back later.' He pressed the red phone icon, ending the call. He crawled quickly over the double bed to where his wife still slumbered. 'Connie, Connie! Wake up.' He continued to shake her slender arm as she grumbled in annoyance at the intrusion upon her sleep.

'For God's sake, Tom, you know that I've got an early start. What is it, what do you want?'

'I'm sorry, love, but you've got to see this on the news… look,' he replied, pointing animatedly at the TV set.

Connie grimaced as she tried to open her sticky eyes. Red hair lay across her pale freckled face as she turned from her warm and comfortable position. 'What's all the fuss, eh?' she asked with irritation. 'Why have you woken me up, what's so important?'

Tom held her soft, 25-year-old face in his hands, and turned her head carefully towards the blinking television screen. He watched Connie's expression change from a tired frown, to one of open-mouthed shock. This seemed to delight him in a strange way, as a nervous grin flashed wide across his good looks.

'Tom, what's going on, is this for real?'

He jumped into the bed next to Connie, placing his legs under the duvet. The young couple both sat staring at the screen, mesmerised as the conference continued.

'Mike Harlowe from Fox News. Mr. President, there has been some satellite disruption coming from Antarctica lately, add to this the significant rise in sea levels due to the massive amounts of the melting ice shelf. I don't know if you are aware of these stats, but are they linked to the ships and their arrival?'

The President patted his greying hair, checking that it was still in place. 'That I can't tell you, Mr. Harlowe. Probably not, though at this stage we can't rule anything out. What I can assure you, and the people of the USA, is that we are doing everything possible within our power to get these answers. As soon as we know, you will know.'

Harlowe shifted his heavy build in the small metal chair. His thick grey eyebrows curled downwards as he lifted an index finger in an attempt to force another question.

The President picked up his papers, looking over the room as his aide approached him. The camera flashes strobed, illuminating the entire room once more. Several questions simultaneously hogged the air as the journalists fought for their leader's attention; Harlowe seemed to drown within the middle of them. The aide placed his arm around the President's side as he led him from the podium, and off camera.

Suddenly, there was a loud electrical crackle. The TV screen changed from the press briefing room, and into a bright white light that forced Tom and Connie to shield their eyes with the backs of their hands. As the light slowly softened, all hands dropped to the bed. Startled, they flung themselves backwards in instinctive fear, only to be met with the rigid blue-cushioned headboard that resurrected their rationality with a thump.

'Yes, Connie, this is for real,' said Tom in a strangely calm manner.

On the screen before them sat the head and shoulders of a bizarre, grey-skinned humanoid being. Its large round black eyes swam amongst its leathery face, along with two minuscule nasal holes that were fixed above a small, thin mouth. Behind it, a black badge made up of red lines and triangles appeared proudly on show. A deep mechanical voice spoke aloud:

'My species have no need to communicate using vocal chords as we use telepathy. However, to convey our message to your world, we wish to make things easier for you. We will be using what you call "digital voice"; our thoughts shall be entered into a machine that will translate them into sound, exactly as you hear now.'

Connie grasped Tom's right hand as the two of them huddled together, shoulder to shoulder. He turned up the volume using the remote control, not once taking his eyes off the intimidating creature that glared back at them as it continued.

'We feel it is necessary to explain to you what is happening. Our species are called the Dextera Domini, though we understand that you have referred to us in the past as the "Greys". The Domini come from a planet far beyond yours, called Dominicus, or what you perhaps perceive as Heaven. Yes, your "Heaven" exists. We have spoken with the various gods of the universe, and all have agreed that the time for your judgement has come.'

The alien's face contorted as it paused; its smooth, yet slimy skin glistened in the white glow. The invisible machine spat out the words which threatened of the world's impending doom.

'Every single human being on this planet shall be judged on their lives, regardless of age or gender. We respect that your laws are only man-made, and the fact that what makes them right or wrong is down to the codes set by humanity. Every planet's laws are different; we have to follow them accordingly as this is how each species live their moral or immoral lives by. This being said, once every single piece of a human's life has been analysed, we shall then commence judgement—and determine which of you will be sentenced to death for your crimes.'

Tom slid a protective arm around Connie. They looked at each other, distraught as their eyes locked. This would no doubt affect them.

'Tom, it says in the Bible that it's a sin to engage in adultery. What's going to happen to us?'

Connie started to cry. He held her where they sat, rocking her soothingly as he stared forlornly out of the window of the 12-storey London apartment block, of which they shared the tenth floor.

'That is different, Connie. Your ex-husband was a cruel and violent man who, if it wasn't for me, would probably have killed you by now.'

She lifted her head slightly, pushing her unruly hair aside from her glazed green eyes. 'I know but—'

'Don't you dare feel bad—I don't. I have loved you from the first time that I met you. I had to watch that bastard treat you like shit for months. If you want to blame somebody, then blame me. I was the one who stole his wife, who took you away from him.'

She lovingly nestled her head into Tom's broad right shoulder. Raising her eyes, she focused them back on the TV screen as the voice continued to speak on behalf of the extraterrestrials.

'Those sinners who are executed shall have their souls transported to Hell, to have due punishments exacted on them. The others, whom we shall call the "inbetweeners", are those who have made minute singular acts. They will be judged on the consequences that their sins have had on their victims' lives. The good shall live, thrive on this Earth amongst each other in peace and tranquility; only when they die naturally will they be presented with the rewards of Heaven, and the paradise that it offers.'

A loud humming shot from the crackling audio of the TV set. Connie jerked in fear at the noise, thrusting her face into Tom's shoulder again as the alien's mouth appeared to speak.

'Those who have been judged as sinners must prepare themselves. We will be transporting ourselves to your living quarters, to remove you for execution and eternal punishment.'

The image of the humanoid disappeared in a static blast of black and white lines. The studio news crew looked to each other, puzzled and alarmed at what they had just witnessed as they became live on air again.

Tom and Connie hugged each other fiercely. The grim warning caused goosebumps to surface all over their skin. He took comfort as he lay his cheek on top of Connie's head; her thick hair cushioned his cheekbones like a copper-coloured pillow, offering childlike reassurance as he closed his eyes and nuzzled his face deep.

'What happens now?' said Connie, her voice slightly muffled. 'Do we run away and hide, hoping that they'll forget about us, or do we carry on as normal? I mean, we should be okay shouldn't we, we're only "inbetweeners", or whatever they called them, right?'

Let's hope so! Tom sighed as the questions burdened his mind. 'I don't know. If we run away, as I imagine many will, then where do we go? If they can transport themselves into our homes, then they must know who we are.' A shiver ran down his spine at the thought. 'We can't rule it out though, running is still an option. We need to wait and see what happens, to see how this plays out before we make any concrete decisions.'

They lay side by side, the duvet cover pulled up to their necks as though it offered protection. Very little sleep followed.

The morning sun was beginning to pierce through the fabric of the dark blue curtains. Its warm glow lit up the room, giving no hint of the shock that was about to hit parts of the waking world.

Tom released Connie, laying her head gently down onto the pillow. He walked barefoot towards the white sash window, pulling back the curtains as he always did, as though the events were all a horrible dream. He looked at the loving photograph of him and his wife, encased in a wooden frame, complete with shells and plastic starfish; it was taken on a holiday to Tenerife two years ago. His lips parted in a half smile as the memory resurfaced, offering a fuzzy warmth within his heart.

The TV news channels continuously replayed the video footage of the spaceships and their arrival. New pictures were sent in by the minute as the updates continued, relentlessly.

He was soon fully awake as the sun glared into his face, forcing him to turn away sharply. Once the white dots had disappeared from his dazzled eyes, he looked back out at the early morning December shine. People hung out from the windows of the adjacent buildings, staring up into the light. Others lined the streets, their eyes again were transfixed upon the cold, yet beautiful sky. As his vision gradually cleared, he inhaled in fright. Dominating the vast skyline were several one and a half mile wide dark metallic discs. Two rows of orange lights circled the crafts' sides. Many smaller ships swam across the city in the distance; their quadrilateral frames glided elegantly through the air. He took several steps back from the large window. Connie watched with one eye open as he sat on the side of the bed, pointing towards the wooden window frame and what lay beyond. The giant circular shapes outside now blocked most of the chilly winter sunlight; their bright panelled bases lit the streets in a clean white luminescent glow.

'What is it, Tom, what's wrong?'

A look of dread passed across his dimly lit features. 'I don't think that we'll be going anywhere,' he proclaimed, defeated. 'I'm sorry.'

The news channels broadcasted more reels of footage as the crafts hung in the skies. From Paris to Moscow, South Africa to Tokyo, alien eyes were everywhere. The chaos and panic had already started as millions flocked to the streets in mass prayer and protest. Other devout religious groups worshipped the menacing shapes that surveyed the globe with sinister intent.

'I think it might be a better idea to stay put for a while anyway,' Tom suggested as he looked to Connie, scratching his head.

'Why? We'll be sitting ducks if we stay.'

He stood and beckoned to his wife to join him at the window, now he had calmed. She obliged as she swung her smooth legs sideways out from underneath the duvet. Her matching grey cotton vest and shorts appeared washed out as flashes of alien light danced across her body. Together they hugged, looking out upon the damned world before them as the streets ran with rivers of terrified people who were already attempting to flee.

'If there really is a God, would he let this happen to us?' asked Connie as she held her hand up to her face, shielding her eyes. She seemed to know the answer already as Tom kissed the top of her head.

'The Bible mentions Judgement Day, and the second coming of Jesus. I assume that the aliens' dawn of a new era—a peaceful planet, that is—shall be the second coming.'He shrugged his shoulders as he thought on this. 'I dunno, maybe Jesus is just terminology for who these creatures are. That being said, there hasn't been any proof that the aliens have actually spoken to God, if of course he even exists?!' He stared out, watching as two men began fighting over a tartan blanket that had been dropped. 'You're right though, Connie. If he does exist, then why? What if this is just a case of extraterrestrials tapping into our fears, you know, masking the truth of an impending invasion?'

Tom frowned, rubbing his forehead with the palm of his right hand as he pondered these thoughts for a second. What if this is all a smoke-screen, though what would be the point? Invasion is inevitable, no matter how you look at it.

'I'd better ring work and tell them that I'm not coming in, though I think that they've probably guessed that by now,' said Connie, now bathed in the white light that lit the streets.

Tom shook his head at her bizarre way of thinking. 'I think you'll find that nobody has gone to work today, except for maybe the emergency services.' He relaxed his hold and turned to her. 'I don't think we should keep standing in this bloody light, we could be swamped in high levels of radiation for all we know.'

She glanced back at him with an immediate look of worry upon her face. Quickly stepping back from the window, she yanked the curtains shut.

Most of the day they sat in the bedroom of their apartment, watching the developments on Sky News, then BBC World News. They flitted between the television screen and the view outside their window as the night began to draw in.

'Have you heard from Vincent since this morning?' Connie suddenly said above the noise of the TV.

Vincent was Tom's oldest friend. They first met at primary school when they were seven years old, and became friends when Vincent had lent him some football socks. They remained close over the last 21 years.

'No, I tried ringing him a couple of hours ago, but he didn't pick up. Maybe he's down there with the crowds, or done a runner to his mum's house. I'll try him again later. I hope everything is okay,' said Tom as he shouted through from the small, boxed-in kitchen. He returned with some hastily made sandwiches, cutting across the room at an angle as he approached his wife.

Connie turned her nose up at the offering. 'No.'

'You've got to eat, love, we need all the strength we can get. I hate to put a downer on things, but for all we know this could be our last meal for a while.'

Connie sighed. She knew he was right, she just didn't want to think that far ahead. She stared at him for a while, her green eyes taking in the saddening expression on his face. She half smiled in gratitude as she took one of the sandwiches, only managing half before tossing it back onto the plate.

Tom picked up the plate from the bed and placed it on the bedside table. He flicked the switch on the lamp; the illumination casting long shadows upon the oceanic blue walls.

'Are you okay, Connie?' he asked as he adjusted the curtains, taking one last look at the black silhouettes that occupied the night. He was greeted with a nervous smile.

BREAKING NEWS! BREAKING NEWS!

He leapt onto the bed next to Connie as the black words flashed across the bottom of the screen on a yellow background. She clasped his right hand to which he responded by caressing the top of hers with his left.

The news presenter, Nick MacMillan, spoke ashen-faced. Despite his fearful tone, he tried to remain professional.

'The process has begun. We understand that the aliens have already started to remove what they call "the sinners" from their homes and surrounding areas. Footage is being sent in from around the world as the abductions are occurring. I warn you that the images you are about to see are distressing.'

The apprehensive presenter paused. A mobile phone video recording played on the TV screen.

A brown-haired teenage boy screams as he runs into his parents' bedroom, all the while filming on his mobile phone as four, extremely tall grey aliens stoop menacingly as they circle the boy's father. His mother, turns to her son, shouting at him to run as she tries to pull at her portly husband. One of the creatures produces a silver pen-like device and points it at the woman. An orange burst of light instantly paralyses her where she stands. Her eyes move from left to right, her mouth dribbling as she struggles to fight the paralysis. The large man is violently attacked with cattle prod-type weapons. The aliens grab him as he falls to his knees onto the coffee-coloured carpet. They all climb out through the high apartment block window. The distraught wife begins to move as the effects wear off from the paralysis. Sobbing, and against her will, she walks straight out of the window, falling 25 floors to her death as her son cries hysterically for her. He runs to the window only to see a smaller, square shaped craft hovering powerfully outside. The woman's crumpled and bloodied body lay—pixellated for the viewers' benefit—on the concrete below.

The news studio remained in silence. Nick raised his tear-filled brown eyes and looked directly down the camera. 'This next clip has just been sent in from Damien Gold, a resident of Frinton-On-Sea, Essex. Again, I must state that some of the images are disturbing.'

The second clip began to play. This time the footage showed another block of apartments, on the South coast, as more square football field-sized ships floated outside the apartments. There, many shadowy alien forms walked in mid-air—many storeys high—along invisible 'bridges' that enabled them to enter their victims' homes. They rounded up the humans, exiting one apartment after another as they marched onto the ship. Screams emanated from within the worn buildings as loved ones were abducted by the creatures. Some went voluntarily, too scared to resist. Others had to be carried or dragged, putting up a fight as best as they could.

Nick twitched uneasily in his black leather swivel chair. 'God have mercy on us all,' he said solemnly as he tried to clear his throat.

Tom and Connie watched open-mouthed, trembling as the videos played on every news channel.

'They're new, we didn't see those ships earlier,' said Tom. 'I think we'd better batten down the hatches, don't you think?'

Connie looked at him, crushed, beaten. 'It won't matter.' She switched her attention back to the news.

'And with me now in the studio is Professor Lawrence Fellberg, Head of Physics at Cambridge University. Welcome, Professor, it's good to have you here with us,' said Nick politely, yet obviously still traumatised by the videos that he had just viewed.

'Thank you,' replied the ginger ponytailed Fellberg, nodding as he spoke.

'This is extremely frightening. What is happening exactly, can you shed any light on proceedings, Professor?'

He nervously twiddled the cuffs of his sand-coloured jacket. 'It's quite simple, Nick. The extraterrestrials—or Greys—appeared in the exosphere before entering our atmosphere.'

'Then why were they not spotted? Why were they allowed to position themselves in key locations like this?'

'They weren't spotted because their ships have an advanced type of cloaking device enabled. These devices allowed them to practically walk right up to the front door and ring the bell.'

'Yes, okay, but surely there must have been some clue, anything? And why did we open the door to them so easily?'

Fellberg appeared angry. 'Look, you've got to understand that we are obviously dealing with a far superior intelligence here. You don't dive into any rash decision. How could we have known that this was their intended plan, we couldn't know—didn't.' The Professor took the questions personally, as though the blame was being laid at his feet. 'The only thing that piqued some mild curiosity was the low signatures from space, picked up by the Hubble Space Telescope.' He narrowed his beady eyes as he stared at Nick. 'Nothing more, nothing less.'

'I actually believe him,' said Connie as the two voices on screen continued to bicker in the background.

Tom looked out of the window, mesmerised. A frost had blanketed the street, glistening under the brightly lit panels. His initial fear at the ships and their arrival still hadn't diminished, though he looked on with just as much awe at the floating discs. He walked away from the window and sat down on the bed.

'I do too,' he said with a sigh. 'We couldn't have opened fire on them without knowing their goals. Can you imagine if we did, and then found that all they ever wanted was peace? Well, we didn't stand a chance either way really.'

Connie held a green elastic hair tie between her lips. 'But everyone knows the truth now, so why hasn't the military done anything?' she mumbled, pulling her generous hair into a thick bunch.

'That's a bloody good question, love. Where are the military?' He stared at the two men on the TV screen, not really listening to what they were saying anymore; he seemed more fixated on the continuous new videos that played. 'The attacks have started, it's not like there's a compromise in this, so why haven't they acted?'

Suddenly, the building began to vibrate. 'Tom,' said Connie, gripping the duvet as she failed to grasp why the room was trembling.

Tom looked down at his feet; the floor seemed to rumble beneath him. He turned to where Connie was to see if she was okay. The stare he received in return was enough as it signalled that she wasn't fine. Ornaments bounced unbroken on the thickly carpeted floor.

Their attention was diverted as several people began shouting as though in argument. Tom stumbled as he made his way towards the windowsill. He grasped it firmly before gazing out through the glass. Shocked, he pulled his head back as an alien craft hovered three floors below.

'Tom,' called Connie again, a look of fear contorting her features.

He raised his hand to suggest quiet, stillness. He slowly lifted the heavy window, delicately sliding it up, and poked his head out through the shuddering, flaking frame.

The voices increased in volume as the sound of large crashes echoed through the flimsy walls and ceilings of the apartments. He started to shake as he watched the Kelvin family—all four of them—forcefully marched out along the unseen bridge, and onto the ship. The father, John, shivered in the icy breeze as the aliens cruelly dragged his bare and bloodied body. Tom closed his eyes for a second, and clenched his fists.

Good on you, John. Looks like you put up a hell of a fight, mate.

Five of the Greys loaded the screaming family on board the craft amidst a humming drone. The two young daughters clung petrified to their mother's arms as they were aggressively pushed towards the orange lit entrance.

Tom, still fascinated by their technology, let his gaze wander along the invisible structure. Looking down, he could see the entire street through the bridge. He watched, captivated as thin veiled ripples shot outwards as the aliens' weight crossed the transparent walkway. People who came out to witness the abductions stood below, looking high up. Their figures wobbled like jelly as Tom stared through the transparent bridge. His eyes followed the line back from the ship, stopping midway. There, one of the aliens had paused, and was staring back at him with an empty expression upon its face. It pointed a spindly finger at him; he studied its smooth face for a few seconds before a chill shot down his spine.

'What's happened, where is that noise coming from?' said Connie, rubbing her arms to keep warm as she moved towards the window.

Tom pulled his head in quickly from the cold. 'It's nothing, you don't need to see this,' he said fiercely as she approached and attempted to look past his head. He rapidly closed the window as the smaller craft took off, the rumblings becoming more distant. He struck the walls twice with the balls of his fists. 'I said leave it!' He tried to hold her back by her shoulders, but it was no use. Connie barged past him, thrusting her face into the glass panels as she tried to see what her husband had just witnessed.

'What did you see? Tell me!' she asked angrily as her breath faded from the glass. Her face flashed a tone of deep red as the blood surfaced in her cheeks. She slid her hands underneath the frame and pushed upwards with force. Her freckled scowl surveyed the freezing darkness for a minute. 'Leave this window open a little bit, we need some air in here.'

'What, so you want them to jump straight in, with no resistance?'

'Tom, just leave it open,' she said flatly, pulling her head back in. 'I don't think a window is going to stop them, do you?'

He thought about it for a second. 'Then keep the bloody heating on, it's bitter out there!'

He placed his arms against the wall, above his head. He could feel the pitted texture of the paint as it pressed against his skin. It was strangely calming, grounding him. He was beginning to worry about Connie. Her bizarre comments gave him the feeling that she wasn't coping well with the events, though to be fair, who was?

'John. It was John and Marie… and the girls, they were all taken,' he said as he rested his damp forehead against his toned arms.

Connie dropped her head as the tears began to form in her eyes. They both knew the family, and liked them. 'Why would they take the kids, what possible things could they have done?' She brushed her arm in an apologetic, yet loving gesture across Tom's back before climbing onto the bed. 'Why?'

'I think it's time, Connie. We need to be ready.'

'I know, I know.' She looked at his strained face for suggestions. 'What do we do?'

Tom gave her an empty look in reply. I don't know the answer to that.

The darkness within the room had begun to close in. The glow from the bedside lamps lit the room in a low level yellow. They both sat on the bed, still watching the incessant stream of video footage that kept flooding in from all over the globe. Tom had tried earlier to find something other than the news to watch, but all other channels had ceased broadcasting. It made sense, he thought. After all, who was going to hang around? Most who worked had probably vacated the city by now anyway.

Nick MacMillan spoke slowly, tiredly. The blank look upon his lined face was one of defeat. The crow's feet etched into the corners of his eyes deepened with each meaningful twitch. He knew that this was potentially the end of civilisation, but he still had a job to do as the black and yellow news tags flowed across the bottom of the screen.

'He looks ill doesn't he,' said Connie, munching on a chocolate biscuit.

Tom was pleased that she was eating, but knew that deep inside his wife had accepted her fate, and this worried him. He placed a reassuring arm around her shoulder, smiling as she gazed at him.

He looked at the alarm clock, it read 17:36 p.m. The sound of grumbling skies had become normal background noise over the course of the last 12 hours. He stood at the window looking out into the white light. The faint, almost non-existent wintery evening desperately strived to penetrate the false brightness that sat over and around the ship. Reddish glows littered the old streets, sputtering out from the worn steel lampposts. Crazed shouts and screams could be heard far and wide. His palms felt clammy as he lay them on the sill; the breeze that shot in under the inch-high window opening felt briefly refreshing against the radiator's heat.

Tom was enjoying the modest serenity as the light flickered around the bedroom. Lone rumbles emanated from afar as glowing dots could be seen scattered across the horizon. Suddenly, a thunderous roar blasted their street as one of the alien crafts descended from the sky at speed. The deafening noise positioned itself directly outside of the apartment, 50 feet away from their window. The whirring mechanical vibrations shook the building, causing dust and dirt to fall all around. The ornaments had fallen to the carpet again, followed by picture frames, some of which broke. The throbbing sensation was beginning to make him feel sick. He placed his hands over his ears as the din grew louder still. Stepping away from the window, he moved towards Connie who sat cross-legged in the middle of the bed. With one hand held out, his fingers jerked backwards then forwards as he beckoned her to follow him, all the while never taking his eyes away from the glass.

A blinding white glow blasted out from the ship, lighting the whole of their bedroom. The beam's filmy surface scoured every nook and cranny as it probed the apartment. It circled, like a lighthouse warning vessels of impending rocks, as it searched high and low.

Tom stood frozen, silent. The light stopped over Connie's trembling face, causing her to close one eye. It crackled with static as it ran a scanning program over her body. Strange red symbols typed themselves out on an invisible screen within the light. Once it had completed its cycle, a smooth digital picture of her face was displayed next to the unique text.

'Tom,' she whispered with fear as she crept backwards from the bed on all fours.

The light then shifted its attention towards Tom. He remained statuesque as the same procedure was repeated over his shaking torso. The cycle again ran its course before his picture was displayed in the same fashion as Connie's. The light then shut itself off. They looked to each other hesitantly, cautiously.

Momentary quiet followed. Bang! The window suddenly shattered, blowing inwards as the vibrations intensified. Tom held up his hand to shield his face from the showering glass. Connie screamed as she planted her head into the duvet. Standing at the foot of the bed, he summoned the courage and peered around the curtains. They flapped furiously from the propulsion system discharges that held the craft aloft.

'Fuck!' he shouted as he danced from foot to foot, 'they're coming, shit, they're coming!'

Connie began crying hysterically. 'Oh no, what do we do?' she said, now scrambling faster across the bed.

Four Greys walked the invisible path to the broken window. Within seconds they were in the room, hunching silently, ready for attack.

'Leave us alone, we haven't done anything wrong!' shouted Tom above the howling breeze as it blew through the broken glass.

Tom grabbed Connie by her hand, pulling her from the bed. They both backed up against the wall, shouting for help as eight outstretched grey arms arrowed towards them... no one was coming. He looked around in desperation as he sought a weapon, anything for protection. His eyes locked onto the empty red coffee mug that sat on the bedside cupboard. Instinctively he picked it up and threw it. The mug struck the nearest alien in the face before dropping to the floor; an aggressive snort left its twitching nasal holes as it shook its head.

'Stay away from us!' he warned as Connie inched slowly behind his back. Tom winced as her nails dug through his white t-shirt and into his skin. He could feel his back quiver as her hands clung on for dear life.

One of the creatures produced a thin gadget. Tom knew that this was the paralysis pen that he had seen earlier on the news. He grabbed the paisley lamp and smashed the device out of the alien hand that intruded upon their space. The instrument dropped to the floor and began rolling underneath the bed, slowing in the rich carpet fibres. The tension from the lamp cord pulled Tom back, causing him to nearly fall as he crashed into the bedside table. The alien retracted its hand like an injured animal, turning to its compatriots as it sought its next set of instructions.

A grey finger pointed outwards before rejoining the rest of its digits in a closed fist; the fist bounced up and down twice in quick succession. The alien turned back from what seemed to be its superior. It moved in closer again, crouching as it readied itself for a second attempt.

Tom raised his left arm to shield Connie, before gently pushing her slim body further behind his own. With his trembling right hand, he ripped the cord from the wall and held the lamp up, waiting to strike the encroaching enemy. The other aliens spread themselves out into a triangle formation, surrounding the disorientated, terrified couple.

He tightened his grip on the lamp's gold base. 'Stay away—I'm warning you!'

Connie was now squeezing Tom's arm so hard that it began to go numb. His dark eyes shot in every direction as he tried to be ready for whichever creature came first. A raspy squeal left the creeping alien's mouth as it attempted to lunge at them. Tom swung hard, crunching the lamp into its large head. The glass cracked into several pieces that flew in all directions. The alien collapsed to the floor, stunned as jagged shards protruded from its skull. Its face grimaced in pain as it gripped the duvet in an effort to rise; a bloody handprint remained upon the cover as it pulled the duvet to the floor. The others all looked at it with curious eyes before turning their attention back to the humans. Long sharp fragments around the lamp's base were all that remained in Tom's shaking hand.

'Come on then!' he raged, swiping the base through the air.

Another Grey leapt forwards like a praying mantis, grabbing at Connie as she let out a horrific scream. Tom turned and stabbed the creature in its neck and arms several times with the broken object. It raised its thin limbs in an effort to protect itself as its brown blood spattered across Tom's animated face.

The alien let go of Connie, staggering as the others became keen to end this. One jumped over the bed sideways, effortlessly landing directly at Tom's left side. Again he attacked the creature, stabbing it repeatedly in a blind frenzy, leaving its leathery torso covered in deep gashes. It backed away, dazed as it touched its bleeding wounds gingerly. It appeared in shock, as though it didn't believe that a weak human could inflict such damage upon itself. The lead alien's face lost its smooth exterior. It looked to the splintered window frame and signalled for them to leave. The injured soldiers struggled, ducking awkwardly through the hanging pieces of wood and glass. They floated out across the air before boarding their vessel.

The alien leader sat on the windowsill, its gangly legs hanging half out as it stared intensely at Tom. Connie released her grip slightly, allowing the blood to circulate back in her husband's arm again. Her eyes gently peered over his shuddering shoulders. He glared back at the creature, disgusted. He spat as he wiped the extraterrestrial blood from his face. He thrust his body forwards in a mock attacking motion. The alien dropped out of the window.

'This isn't over Connie, this is far from over,' he said quietly.

Connie looked into Tom's eyes, squinting as she studied them carefully. She gently prised what was left of the bloodied lamp from his stiff fingers, and placed it on the bedside cupboard. She was unnerved by the man who now gazed back at her. Gone was the warm and friendly kindness that had once accompanied his good looks, that had often drawn her into his strong arms. It was now replaced by a harshness that seemed empty, devoid of any feeling. She hugged him, never wanting to let go; his firm arms wrapped around her. Connie closed her eyes. She felt a tiny glimmer of the man whom she adored come flowing back—he was still in there somewhere.

Tom stood next to the window, peering out through the thin gap that separated the curtains. The misshapen pieces of wood that he had taped to the crudely repaired frame to replace the broken glass, wobbled as a strong breeze blew through its shallow material. Shouts echoed from the streets as more people were taken against their will. He looked through the cracks, up to the skies. He sighed in defeat. The dotted bright lights could be observed across the whole city for as far as he could see. My God, there must be thousands of people being taken.

Connie ran from the bathroom in her baggy red robe. Tom smiled tiredly as he watched her towel dry her unruly hair. They hadn't talked about what had happened earlier with their attempted abduction; he felt that it was bad enough to think about it, let alone talk about it. Besides, he had had to calm her when she broke down in floods of tears, frantically ripping the blood-stained duvet cover from the bed. He felt it best to leave her be for now.

Screams continued to shred their nerves as a ship attacked the building in the next street. Peeping out again, Tom stared at the silhouettes of the houses that sat beneath the vibrating craft. Now and again a faint light caught the stones and their 1970's style cement exteriors, showing the dull designs in all their old-fashioned glory. The houses seemed small, Tom thought, as he casually watched a young African woman pleading as she desperately fought to prevent the aliens from dragging her off—it didn't work.

BREAKING NEWS! LIVE! BREAKING NEWS! LIVE!

The television flashed as Nick MacMillan appeared on screen in his now crumpled grey suit. His voice continued as the cameras streamed live to their feed.

'Tom, you'd better see this,' Connie said, glancing quickly towards the window.

The two of them faced the TV. Tom shuddered as he heard the craft outside ascend into the night, knowing that the helpless woman was onboard.

'We have breaking news for you, er ... yes, here we are,' said Nick as he pressed his right hand against his plastic earpiece. 'Yes, we can go live to New York City, and what you are seeing here is the President of the United States, and the British Prime Minister. It appears they are leaving the United Nations Headquarters. We can only assume that the UN leaders have all been present, but we're not quite sure what is going on. As you can see, they are walking together, flanked by four security advisors as they head towards one of the alien ships that remains stationary.'

The craft let out a dramatic hiss, causing the watching crowds present to cower in gasps of shock.

'A door has opened on the ship. I can't quite see inside, but—ah, there is movement. Six Greys have exited and are approaching the leaders. The security are doing their jobs well, cautious, though nervous under these circumstances, which is completely understandable given the situation.'

The stress had taken its toll on Nick MacMillan's face. The last 24 hours seemed to have aged the man 10 years overnight. He looked gaunt as he commentated on the unusual proceedings that were unfolding. He once again held two fingers against his earpiece. 'I'm being informed that we can now go to our North American correspondent, Carol Thirston. Carol, can you hear me?'

The wind blazed powerfully as the blonde-haired young woman tried to keep her light green jacket hood up. The camera quickly fixed on her position. 'Yes, Nick, I can hear you. This is all very bizarre behaviour; we are not allowed too close to the ship that landed no more than 200 feet from us, around five minutes ago. The police are still trying to maintain professionalism, but as you can—'

Tom turned to Connie. 'What the hell is going on?' he asked, perplexed by the whole scenario. 'You can't let them enter that ship, they'll never return!' He held his hands out, gesturing as though he was holding a heavy weight. 'That's what you have aides for, to do the leaders' jobs for them while they are tucked up safe in their underground bunkers.'

He scratched at his unkempt hair before sliding his right hand down and around his day's facial stubble. He moved towards the top of the bed and plumped up his pillow. Connie held his hand as he laid next to her. He loved the feel of her soft fragrant skin as it navigated its way through his fingers, interlocking with them. They continued to stare at the TV screen with a silent apprehension.

Carol stared down the camera. 'The humans are now flanked by the six creatures, who seem to have weapons of some type.' Rain began falling fiercely, its needle-like texture battering her small attractive face. 'I can't really make them out, but I have to say that I don't like the look of this,' she said as she tried to turn her head from the relentless blasts.

A group of protesters began chanting in unison as they came into the camera's line of sight. 'Leave aliens, leave! Leave aliens, leave!' They waved their cardboard signs furiously around the flinching reporter. A shaven-headed man preached from behind Carol's back. 'Who are they to decide who lives and who dies? What gives them the right?' he shouted into her ear as he prodded his finger towards her, forcing her to cringe away from the aggression.

Tom couldn't take his wide-eyed stare from the TV screen. 'Why are they allowing them to set foot on that bloody craft, is it some sort of sacrifice?' he suggested chillingly.

'I don't know, but whatever it is they must know what they're doing, right?' replied Connie. She began running a pink plastic hairbrush through her thick curls. 'I mean, they will have their respective Vice

President and Deputy Prime Minister to take over in any event. But I agree, this doesn't make sense.'

Tom pursed his lips as his brain ticked over for a second. 'Even if it is some sort of peace meeting—negotiations, for example—you wouldn't send your country's leader into a blindfolded situation such as this.'

'Maybe you were right first time; maybe they have offered themselves up in a bid to prevent more bloodshed,' she supplied. 'Anyway, forget about that for now. Go take a shower, it'll make you feel better. And change that t-shirt, I can see the sweat stains underneath the arms from here!'

Tom frowned, oblivious to Connie's remarks. 'Hmmm, I don't know. Besides, there's no way that us and the Yanks would lay down and do nothing.' He tapped the remote control against his right thigh. 'Perhaps they've been captured, and this is the only dignified way of them agreeing to go, rather than being forcibly paraded in front of the world.'

The pictures on the wall suddenly began to rattle. Tom jumped up from the bed and leapt towards the window. He gently used two fingers to slowly part the curtains, and carefully gazed through gaps in the flimsy plywood. 'Oh God!' he shouted as the alien's musty breath struck his face through the cracks in the cheap board. The wood snapped in half as the creature's head burst through the frame. Its dark eyes oozed violence as more Greys followed behind it. He struggled to stay on his feet as he stumbled backwards. 'Connie, get back up against the wall, NOW!'

She jumped up with a start, and looked to Tom who himself backed up with speed and efficiency as he regained his balance.

'Tom, they're coming, look!'

'I know, I know!' he replied furiously.

Something caught his eye as he joined Connie at the wall. Under the bed, the tip of the alien paralysis device poked out from within the shadow of the uncovered duvet. The creatures began stepping through what was left of the window frame, one after the other. He debated whether he could grab the instrument in time or not. Without a word he took the chance. He sprang forwards—hitting the soft carpet as he landed on his knees—and scooped the gadget up in his right hand.

Four aliens stood tall in the bedroom, bent slightly below the off white painted ceiling. The leader of the group took a step back as the others began their familiar advances.

'Come on, come on you piece of E.T. crap, WORK!' shouted Tom, panicking as he struck the weapon several times against the palm of his left hand.

With his right hand trembling he pointed the device at the group, and began thrusting it outwards as he desperately tried to make it work. Suddenly, his hand jerked on its own as tiny lights on the weapon's stem glowed in a yellow sequence. They all paused and looked at the gadget, waiting. The aliens started to move away from him as the lights reached their peak. Tom, sensing their hesitancy, took a step forward. The weapon squirted out an odourless, mustard-coloured vapour that engulfed the humanoid in front of him.

Tom looked at the instrument in his hand with raised eyebrows. A new urgency now had a hold of him as the being collapsed to the floor, motionless. Its small quivering lips were the only signs that it was still alive. The others began retreating hastily.

'Yeah, you fucking know it!' Tom said with an air of bravado.

He raised his right arm at the next alien, clenching his teeth as he prepared to strike. From his left came a large shadow that knocked the device out of his hand. It flew into the wall with a dense thud before hitting the floor where it buzzed and sparked, broken.

Tom grappled with the alien; the feel of its slimy skin in his hands made his stomach turn. Its oval eyes bore down on him as it over-whelmed his strength, forcing him down to his knees.

Connie let out a horrendous cry. Tom looked over to where his wife was, grimacing as he fought the alien hard. She struggled to evade the two monsters who had a violent hold of her. He watched as terror crept over her pretty features. The aliens twisted her arms hard, al-most breaking them as she begged them to stop. In a split second, the immense love he felt for her washed over his soul. He stared blankly as they began to pull her towards the window frame, kicking and screaming. A bizarre feeling of doom dominated him—he could feel the end coming.

The alien looked deep into his eyes. Give up pathetic human, your time is at an end!

The fight began to disappear from his limbs as he started to lose all hope.

'Tom… Tom!' screamed Connie as the Greys dragged her by her arms.

Her shrill voice brought him back to reality. All the noise in the room became crystal clear. The creature's moist face stopped an inch from his own sweaty, agonised features. He could see his feeble reflection within the huge, shiny black eyes.

He loosened his aching arms, releasing his grip from the alien's bony wrists. Sensing victory, it relinquished its own firm hold to one arm. Tom seized his chance. With his free arm he threw it forwards, plunging his fingers into its left eye. The being let out a coarse yelp before smashing the side of Tom's head, knocking him to the floor. The alien clasped its wounded face as thick liquid trickled down and through its spidery fingers.

Tom felt a vital advantage. He grabbed the alien by its ankles, holding on as he rolled over onto his side. Pulling the creature off balance, it fell head first, crashing to the carpet. It lay next to him on its stomach, disorientated; its arms splayed out in front of it, twitching like thin grey branches.

The other Grey that had been paralysed now began to stir as the effects of the spray began to wear off. Time was of the essence. Tom pulled over the small black metal waste bin that sat next to the bed. He tore the plastic bagful of litter from it. Dangling it awkwardly in front of his face, he quickly emptied the assorted contents from it, watching as the junk food wrappers floated to the floor. An empty fizzy drinks can bounced softly; several drops of cherryade leapt onto the carpet, next to the alien blood; its red colour darkening the lighter shade beneath it.

He straddled the alien, placing his legs either side of its torso. He could feel its small ribcage protrude from underneath its skin as he placed the crinkled bag over its head; it was a tight fit, but it worked as the creature began fighting for air. He crossed his hands and held the plastic handles with force. It kicked as it fought for its life. Tom hung on for all his worth, riding the alien's back in desperation. He kept glancing over at the Grey that was coming around, staring with fear as it woke more with each passing second.

'Come on, die you fucking monster, die!'

A final flurry of life burned out rapidly as Tom looked into the alien's eyes. A last breath exhaled from its dry mouth, causing the bag to expand slightly. A tinge of sadness forced the hairs on the back of his neck to rise as he watched the shine of life dissipate. Without hesitation, he left the corpse and climbed to his feet. He stumbled over to the recovering alien that was trying to haul its tall frame upwards. All guilt had quickly disappeared—a swift kick to the body sent it reeling with a gurgling whine; its mouth bent downwards as it experienced pain. For the first time Tom finally got a feel for the extraterrestrials—and they were afraid. With a wild fury he brought down his right foot upon the creature's skull, stamping it until its cranium folded in a mess of blood and brain. Breathing heavily, he looked down upon the mush before him. It reminded him of when he was a child, smashing pumpkins to a pulp during Halloween nights. There was no sentiment now as the gooey liquids soaked into the carpet's thick fibres.

Connie couldn't move as the two Greys gripped large chunks of her hair. They began to slide through the window frame, brutally hauling her out with them. Tom looked around until his eyes met with the oak wardrobe. Without thought he pulled a wire coat hanger that dangled precariously from the top of the half-inch open door. He let out a cry as he ran at the humanoids, his feet leaving bloodied prints across the floor.

He stretched high as he flung the hanger over the alien's neck, pushing and pulling as it stumbled uneasily. It let go of Connie's hair, its face tightening as it tried to grasp at the ligature around its long neck.

They both crashed into the wall with a sickening force; Tom nearly lost his grip as his head bounced off the plaster. The creature clawed at the air as it tried and failed to remove the wire; its fingers couldn't force their way underneath the metal. With a hefty push they both flew towards the window. Tom let go of the hanger as he tried to stop himself from following suit. He staggered in his tracks, watching as the alien grabbed at the blue curtains before it fell head first through the frame. It passed the transparent bridge, and plummeted to its death.

A few cheers surfaced from the remaining residents of the surrounding buildings as the being slammed the concrete path with a bone-crunching thud. The lead alien stood in the width of the frame; even though it was thin, it still seemed to engulf the space as it held Connie by her left arm. It produced one of the cattle prod-type weapons and jabbed it against her freckled skin. The golf ball-sized curved steel end glowed red, and a popping noise came from the instrument. The smell of burning flesh wafted through the apartment. Tom stepped closer as she collapsed, a weakened, dead weight. The creature hoisted her up to her feet. She moaned at the vice-like grip upon her scarred flesh.

The anger swelled throughout Tom's body. 'LET—HER—GO!' he demanded through gritted teeth.

The alien bent down as it pushed its head backwards out through the window. It snarled as it looked to Connie before turning back to Tom. Guilty!

'No, no, no! Don't you dare, please don't do it!' pleaded Tom as the creature's word sank into his mind. Stunned, he raised his shaking hands in surrender. He began to back away, giving the alien some space. It looked directly into his watery eyes, almost mockingly. Tom could have sworn that he saw its lips curl into a slight smile. In one effort it swung its arm fully, sending Connie flying out of the window and into the false light. 'NO!'

In a flash, the alien had lowered its head and jumped out onto the transparent bridge. Tom lumbered towards the frame in a stupor.

Clenching the sill, he thrust his head out into the freezing air. His face was filled with dread.

'Tom…!' wailed Connie as her flailing figure became ever smaller.

Her cry for him echoed around the buildings. He watched in horror as she reached out for him before landing on the path, mangled. Blood slowly pooled around her head, entwining with the alien that lay by her side as she stared back up at him with glassy eyes—she was gone.

'Oh my God, you bastard!' His voice cracked into weak sobs. He put his hands on his pulsating head, pulling at his hair. Previous cheers had now turned to stunned gasps as the residents looked on, devastated. He glared at the alien who shifted backwards along the invisible bridge. 'Why?' he asked as the creature moved further away towards its ship.

Why not?

The words that bled into Tom's mind would forever be imprinted there. He stood, a broken man, as the being disappeared into the ship's orange entrance. He watched silently—distraught—as its propulsion systems kicked in with a whirring force. The blast slammed into the brick face of the apartment block as the ship turned. Its force shot through the broken window frame, hitting his face. He turned his head to a 45° angle, looking through squinted eyes as the craft flew straight up into the darkness.

Chapter 5

Lost Hopes and Plans

A sadness crawled around the room as the remaining humans clung to the wall. James discreetly wiped the tears from his face with the balls of his hands, trying not to show a softness in front of the others. John sat staring at the floor, occasionally lifting his head to glance at each of them. The General was solid, continuously in survival mode as he rubbed his large hands together, seeking warmth. Mark played with the thin mist, teasing it with his fingers, fascinated as it trailed after their lead.

'We're not getting out of here alive, I know this now,' said John, resigned to the fact.

'You don't know that, son,' replied Hargreaves in his gravelly tone. 'Besides, I don't want to hear that shit! While we are alive there is always the possibility of escape.'

John averted his gaze, looking back at the floor.

Mark watched the mood deteriorating. 'Hey,' he whispered towards John.

John lifted his brown eyes in the Professor's direction. Mark gestured with his head, nodding at James' shivering body sitting on the cold floor. John shuffled up next to him; realising that he wasn't the only one that was suffering. He placed his thick arm around James' shoulder, reassuring the youngster that he wasn't alone. Mark showed his appreciation with a wink of his right eye. Heavy sighs continued to abound within the cold atmosphere of the room.

'Are they going to give us any food?' said John, clutching his stomach as it grumbled loudly. 'I'm starving.'

'I wouldn't hold out any hope of food. If we do get fed—and that's a big if—well, it won't be cheeseburgers and fries,' warned Hargreaves in a grim seriousness. 'Expect starvation, as this will no doubt be their next plan of action. Without energy, we're finished.'

'We're finished already,' said John, looking straight into the General's face.

Hargreaves shook his head disapprovingly. 'I know this is going to sound crude, but does any of you have a container, of some description?'

Mark looked around at the others. 'No, I don't think so. Why?'

'We are going to need hydration—our urine might be our only hope of survival.'

'I'm not drinking piss!' said John, alarmed, his head flying back in shock.

Hargreaves shot the man a hard glare. 'You will if you want to live!'

'It's not going to work anyway,' said Mark, his eyelids half closed. 'We don't have any containers or lids, so it's not a solution.'

The four of them once again sat in silence. The room had dropped a degree or two more over the last half hour. Only Mark seemed to notice this, blowing his breath into his clasped hands. He again stared at the others before his eyes wandered, mesmerised, as the soft light scattered the plain walls in patches of weak orange.

'Funny, I always thought that extraterrestrial materials would feel, well, extraterrestrial?!' said Mark as he ran his smooth hand over the clammy wall.

'It's steel, Mark,' said Hargreaves with a curl of his top lip as though the statement had offended him. 'What did you expect?'

The Professor coursed his fingers over the texture before gently rubbing them together.

'What is it?' asked John as he raised his head from within the shadows.

'Nothing. It's just that as a kid you think of "ships from other worlds", and you expect their matter to be different, you know, due to their supposed technological superiority.' He placed his fingers back on the surface of the wall. 'Maybe the materials are the same, who knows?'

They all looked at the walls as best as they could in the poor light.

John ran his hands over the steel. 'Feels raised, a bit like old-fashioned artex.'

'Yeah, I know what you mean,' replied Mark as he gazed to the ceiling, 'it's that pattern-type feel to it. I wonder how they made it, compressed it. I wonder if they have similar machines to ours, that do the same jobs?'

Hargreaves shrugged his shoulders. He had by now given up on constantly dusting off his clothing. He was tired. The last few hours had taken their toll, making him look and feel even older than his already 60 odd years. He lay his head against the wall; he could feel the coolness penetrate through his hair to his scalp. The glow illuminated the flecked stubble upon his face, making it sparkle with every movement.

Mark saw this. He knew why they all failed to keep a routine. But someone as proud as Hargreaves, giving up on his uniform? That was worrying. Deep down he hoped that the General wasn't starting to flag, as without his knowledge and grit, the group would collapse—and he didn't have the strength to do the job himself.

James climbed to his feet. 'Food?! Is that all you lot can think about?' he said, throwing his hands up in the air. 'Tom has just been taken God knows where, and for what sick purpose we don't know, and you're moaning because you're hungry?'

'It wasn't meant like that, James, you know that,' said Mark as he attempted to diffuse the situation.

James placed his hands over his head, interlocking his fingers tightly as he began to pace the room. 'This has got nothing to do with you, Mark. Stay out of it!'

'Really? Let me tell you how I feel.' Mark rose to his feet. 'Just because I act calm, it doesn't mean that I am! Tom has gone and I'm gutted, yet I'm trying my hardest to keep it together, not only for my own sake, but for the group's. I know that if I fold, then I'm no use to anyone—another dead weight.' He pointed his finger at James, and moved closer towards the teenager. 'Has it ever occurred to you that I'm constantly wondering who's next? Knowing that if I'm the last to go there's still no escape, that I'm only prolonging the inevitable, eh? And if I'm last, there'll be no one left and I'll be on my own. Let me tell you, it scares the shit out of me. So don't go you go thinking that you're the only one suffering!'

The others dropped their heads.

James went almost nose to nose with the Professor. 'You think that none of us are thinking the same, Mark?' he said, 'I'm fucking terrified!'

Hargreaves shifted his heavy build in between the two squabbling men. 'Stop this bullshit and pull yourselves together, you're supposed to be men!' he shouted, straight to the point. 'While we are alive there's always a way.'

The two of them looked to the General. His tough stare made them feel like they were young boys being scolded by their strict father. 'Where the hell did that come from, Mark?' he smirked, singling out the Professor. They looked away, ashamed. Hargreaves hovered, waiting for the mood to settle before they all dispersed several feet apart.

'Do you think there are other ships, with other humans on them?' John asked, yawning as he changed the subject.

'Who knows? For all we know we could be the last of the human race,' replied James, his mouth bending downwards. 'Maybe the Earth has gone.'

'Don't be stupid.' Hargreaves stood straight, pushing his barrel-shaped chest out like a strutting peacock. 'I guarantee you that the Earth and the human race are alive and fighting.'

'Yeah,' agreed Mark confidently for the benefit of the group. 'The leaders of the world will still be holding their respective cabinets together somewhere.'

'He's right,' added Hargreaves. 'As I said, while there's life there's fight.'

'But how do you know?' said James with a shrug of his slim shoulders. 'We could be here because the planet has gone; we could even be just a few of thousands of other humans on this ship, we did hear other voices after all.'

The others looked back to the floor, each silently pondering the possibilities.

John sat with his arms wrapped around his body. The rolled-up fur hood of his parka jacket was tucked snug against his neck, offering some warmth against the chill. He stroked his greasy hair repeatedly. Dark marks underlined his eyes as he looked up at Hargreaves. 'How long have you been in the military, General?'

Hargreaves slowly turned his head in John's direction. '43 years. I left school at 16 and signed up—it was the best thing that I ever did. They taught me to be the man that you see today. I've seen it all: wars, the world, the amazing wildlife, everything.'

'Are you married, do you have a family?' James asked, joining the conversation.

Hargreaves' tone deepened. 'No. My wife died several years ago, so I went from semi-retirement back into full swing. We never had children. Marie always wanted them, but now I see that it was a blessing.'

'A blessing?' said James as he shook his head. 'What do you mean?'

'He means that with all that's happened, he hasn't got kids out there to worry about—there are no threats to be used against him,' said Mark as he cut in.

A glaze appeared over Hargreaves' eyes. 'Precisely.'

John raised his eyebrows at the admission. 'What a tragic line of thought.'

'Why is that tragic? If it comes to the crunch I won't be the one spilling the beans on anything. I don't know about you lot, but this is the point; I have nothing to lose, nothing to be taken which can give them an advantage over me. Besides, I've been trained in how to cope with torture in every possible scenario.'

'Fair play, General, fair play. But you're forgetting one thing,' said John with a wry smile across his round face. 'This isn't your standard scenario. This is the likes of nothing that anyone has ever seen before.'

Hargreaves coughed as the mist gathered in his throat. 'Military procedures are one and the same, whoever the enemy.'

John rolled his eyes. 'General, I mean no disrespect, but surely you can't be that naïve? None of us know the type of torture that these fuckers might have in store for us; I'm sure it will involve alien technology of some description. God forbid that they decide to use it on us,' he said with an air of caution as he placed his head against the wall. 'Mark, am I right?'

All eyes turned to the Professor. Mark looked from side to side. 'Don't ask me,' he said as he tried to pull himself out of the conversation. 'I know no more than you do.'

'Come on, Mark, you're the expert. What would you say?' pressed John.

Mark sighed. 'I'm going to have to sit on the fence here. I agree with the General—military procedures are normally the same, whoever you're up against. But I also agree with you, John. No one can be trained for events such as these, they're impossible to predict.'

Hargreaves smiled. Who's naïve now?

John tutted as he rolled his eyes again. 'Good job, Mark, you're a great help.'

'Forget it, I'm not taking sides. I only offer my opinions,' replied the Professor as he ran his hands through his thick hair. The shadows cast his height against the wall, making his silhouette look down upon the others through the haze. 'Sorry, but you asked.'

James sat quietly, he hadn't said much over the course of the last hour. 'Are you alright?' asked Mark.

'As well as anyone can be in this situation, I guess,' came the exhausted reply. He scratched his head before pulling his jacket cuffs back over his hands. 'I'm starting to retrieve pieces, you know, of what happened before we wound up here.'

'Really? That's good, isn't it?'

'Yes and no. I mean it's good to get the truth, yet there are some things that have happened that I don't wish to remember. It's only fragments though, could be mixed in with what other people have said.'

'Such as?'

James shut his eyes firmly for a moment; then opened them wide, stretching the skin around them with the base of his palms. 'I keep getting this feeling of family. It was what the General said, about not having kids? It got me thinking about myself, but it was all a blur. Now I keep getting these images in my head of ...'

'Go on,' said Mark with a gentle nod of his head.

'A sister, I've been getting vague images of having a sister. Things like childhood, short blasts of playing together in a garden, stuff like that.'

'That's great, James. It gives you hope, it gives us all hope.'

Hargreaves suddenly lost his cool. 'If you are playing happy memories, keep them to yourselves!'

'Now come on, General,' said James, obviously annoyed.

Hargreaves pointed aggressively at James, his finger wagging back and forth. 'How many times have I got to tell you people? These grey bastards are more than likely watching us, listening somehow. Keep your shit to yourself, and that goes for all of you. They are most likely taking all of this down to use against you.'

A sympathetic expression crossed Mark's face. 'He's right, James.'

'Fuck you! If I've got a sister out there—any family at all—then I need to know that they're alright.'

Mark placed his hand upon James' shoulder. 'Calm down, we're only trying to help you. What you do affects all of us, we have to be smart.'

Hargreaves flung his arms into the air. 'That's what I've been saying all along for Christ's sake!'

Mark threw Hargreaves a cold stare. 'Yes, General, you've made your point.'

John's whispering voice came shooting through the air as his face came into view. 'I've had enough of this, General. What can we do, tell us what you want from us?' he asked. 'We've got to get out of here, we haven't got a choice anymore.'

The others looked to John, and then to Hargreaves. Cautiously, the General moved to the back wall. He subtly gestured with his eyes for them all to follow his lead.

'Okay. When those bastards last came into the room, did any of you notice if they had any weapons on them?' he whispered quietly.

Their heads closed in together.

'No, I don't recall seeing anything,' replied John. 'It's only been hand to hand combat, I didn't see any weapons strapped to their bodies.'

Hargreaves looked to the others. 'Anyone else?'

'No, you?' said Mark as he looked to James.

Hargreaves got them to remain standing, not too close, but enough distance between them so as not to arouse suspicion. 'We need a plan,' he said, partially covering his mouth to hide what he was saying. 'We know that by causing havoc in here—banging on the walls like Tom did—they will come immediately.' He then wiggled his fingers, suggesting that they all cover their mouths. 'I think that we can take them down, problem is where do we go once we're out of the door? As you've seen yourselves, the corridor runs a short length to the end. But do we go left, or right?'

'Why are we covering our mouths?' asked John curiously, looking round at the dark faces.

'So they can't lip read what we're saying,' said James.

'They can't do that through the mist, it's too hazy. You're just being paranoid.'

'Just do as I do,' said Hargreaves, now becoming frustrated. 'Pretend you're scratching your chin, your stubble, anything … Not too obvious though.'

'So which way did Daniel go?' asked John, now rubbing his chin.

'Either way it didn't do him any good, did it,' said Mark. 'This needs serious thought.'

'You're right, Mark, but our options are limited,' said Hargreaves. 'We have no idea what is waiting for us at the end of that corridor. Christ, Daniel might not have even made it past the end for all we know! Add to this that we have no idea the size of this ship, and how many corridors, well, you get the idea.'

'Yeah, could be like running through a maze, except that this maze is filled with aliens that want to kill you!' said Mark, almost jovially at the ridiculous sounding statement.

'Okay, but how do we find out how big the ship is? It's not like we can go walkabout is it. Even I know that a military tactic would be to send out a scout to test the waters, so to speak,' said James. He waited anxiously for Hargreaves' response.

'You're spot on, James. This would be the first and natural choice, but who's going to go on the scouting mission?'

John chuckled gently. 'Whoever goes is going to die, just like Daniel. So what good would this do, right?' he said with a hint of sarcasm, yet truth. 'It's not like anyone's going to be able to run around the entire ship and report back is it?'

The triangle lit up once again. Its red glow danced upon the wall as its beam blasted powerfully through the mist. Fear was palpable; stifled whimpers echoed as the group waited, shuffling together watched without blinking as the panel ran through its common sequence.

'Stand tall people!' ordered Hargreaves as he readied himself for battle. 'We're about to find out the answers to our questions.'

The door whizzed open. Three Greys again stood in the high frame before entering the room. Their smooth heads peaked above portions of the haze, scanning the room robotically for their captives. This time they held small metallic weapons, like cylindrical stun guns. The group herded together as the aliens prodded the crackling electrical devices through the mist. With a speed that wasn't expected of their build, two of the creatures moved in and grabbed the General.

'Come on then you slimy bastards!' Hargreaves raged as they gripped his arms.

He fought them hard. Limbs flailed wildly as Mark and John grasped at his blazer. The General's age was beginning to show as the effort sapped his strength, weakening him. His tough body loosened somewhat as the aliens gained control of the fight.

'Watch those fucking things, John!' warned Mark as the third alien drove its weapon towards them. 'They must have been listening somehow.'

'Do you think?' shouted John as he leapt forwards then backwards. 'That's what we need, weapons.'

'Then get the bloody things!' cried Hargreaves as he forced himself to fight harder.

The two men tried to evade the oncoming attack as the device was jabbed at them. James stood hunched behind them.

'James, help us,' begged John as he glanced to where the young man had frozen.

A loud crackling buzzed through the air followed by a gurgling cry. One of the Greys had attacked the General in the neck with the weapon, sending a massive static shock through his large bulk. He dropped to his knees as the others looked on. The alien grasped him by the throat—watching with fascination as the veins bulged. Its fingers almost met each other as they squeezed ever tighter round the rough skin of his neck. Its interest soon piqued as it slammed the General's head into the wall.

The glimmer of life in his eyes slowly fizzled out like the orange embers of a hot rock, cooling as the heat no longer surged through it. A tiny breath left his broken jaw, which hung at a repulsive 45° degree angle. The alien repeated its action, and smashed the human's head back into the wall—harder. It stared curiously at the side of the cracked, bashed-in skull. Blood poured from the wounds, racing down the crea-

Chris Botragyi

ture's hand that still forcibly held the pulverised throat. It sniffed cautiously at the red liquid, carefully turning the General's body around as it inspected the resulting damage.

Blood and brain fragments trickled down the wall, mixing with the dusty floor like a thick lentil soup. Unfortunately, the others were close enough to witness the carnage; they looked on, terrified. The gaping holes in the General's head spilled all of his remaining humanity. His life, his soul—and his memories—slid away in a collapsed pile of bone and organ. Another snap and buzz to the General's shoulder jolted his body; it was as if the creatures were expecting him to awake. The Grey dropped the corpse to the grating like a discarded piece of trash.

'General!' shouted Mark as he looked to Hargreaves, and then to the alien that faced him.

The creatures circled the body as they gazed at its weak shell, before slowly backing off. The leader of the three stared towards the being that had killed the General; it responded by grasping the human's right foot and pulling the body out of the door with ease. Hargreaves' glassy eyes looked back at the remaining three humans—the fear had finally overcome the tough soldier. The harsh lined features were frozen in time upon his glistening red face.

The door slid across, cutting off the rest of the corridor. A mixed trail of blood, brains and bone was all that remained of the General. Insects could be heard scampering across the floor as they investigated the scent. They lapped up the nourishing feed with voracity, consuming every part of the messy remains.

Mark slumped to the floor. He knew that their best chance of survival had greatly diminished. 'That's it, it's over,' he said, covering his face with trembling hands.

John placed his hands upon his head as he paced the floor nervously. 'What do we do now?' He looked to Mark. 'We're dead, we're fucking dead!'

'We were dead anyway,' said James, raising his voice. 'They've got what they wanted—we've entertained them.' He curled up in the corner, holding his knees loosely to his chest. 'Why we ever thought that we could escape, it's beyond me.'

'Yeah, like you helped!' said John, looking angrily at the shivering ball.

'Stop it, both of you. Let me think,' said Mark as he held his hands up in front of him.

James rubbed his head with both hands. 'Mark, let it go. You've just said yourself that it's over. There's nothing to think about—it's done, finished.' His eyes were full of tears as he looked up at the Professor. 'Anything we do from this point forward is futile.'

An aggressive sneer dominated John's face. 'What the fuck is wrong with you?'

'Leave it, John.' Mark squatted against the wall. He placed his elbows upon his knees, and balanced his forehead on the tips of his fingers. 'He's right, we're finished. Our best chance—if there ever was a chance—has just gone out of that door in a pile of mush.'

Chapter 6

Interview with an Alien—The General's Story

The room was dark but for the bright spotlight, and red dot that glowed from the video camera. The camera's metal tripod cut an imposing figure as it stood dominantly, proud in the corner. A basic brown wooden desk took centre stage in the room. Thick cigarette smoke swirled in the air—its dance mesmerising to the grey being that sat on one side of the desk. Several military personnel including scientists and doctors, muttered amongst themselves. They all stared, intrigued, through the four-foot wide rectangular one-way mirror that adorned the wall opposite the desk. Three silhouettes sat guarded.

'My name is General James F. Hargreaves, and for the benefit of the camera's audio it is 11.49 a.m. Wednesday 24th September, 2012. Sat to my left is the head of the Theoretical Physics Department, Dr. Steven Hatfield.' The General gestured towards his young blonde-haired colleague. Hatfield in turn nodded his acknowledgement as he gazed at the large black oval eyes before him. 'I suppose the first question would be to ask where you are from?' said Hargreaves in a deep, yet upbeat husk.

The alien being cocked its large round head to one side. Its leathery skin seemed to wrinkle, then tighten momentarily.

Hargreaves shook his head sharply as though regaining focus. 'So, I have just established that you can communicate by telepathy, which is astounding.' He took off his hat and placed it carefully on the table in front of him, desperate to avoid any contact with whatever dust lay on the formica surface. 'For the record though, can we please all speak out aloud? Thank you.'

The alien looked at Hargreaves. A blank, emotionless stare drank in the General's solid build that betrayed his years. The only giveaway were the ageing lines in the rough skin that framed his square jaw. His cropped, receding silver hair sprouted like prickles over his head.

Again, the alien leant its head to one side. 'It's irrelevant where I am from, but let me ask you: where are we?' it said in a vibrating humanoid tone. It looked around the smoky room cautiously. 'I can't tell as you all blank your thoughts around me when entering this structure.'

Hatfield couldn't work out if the alien was looking around in curiosity or fear, though he suspected it was more likely the former. The Doctor sat hunched, his soft clean fingers intertwined in front of him. He was fascinated as he gazed at the way the alien's skin folded, looking smooth yet slightly wrinkled.

'I see that you are as curious to my appearance, as am I to yours, Dr. Hatfield,' said the alien as it turned its heavy head towards the doctor.

Hatfield shifted his slim body uneasily in the collapsible metal chair. He seemed hypnotised by the alien's eyes; they reminded him of hard black onyx stones.

Hargreaves coughed into his thick fist as he interrupted, sensing that the interview was rapidly falling apart. 'Well, we are at Groom Dry Lake Air Force Base, Nevada. It is a heavily restricted area, known more commonly—or referred to—as Area 51.'

The alien focused its attention back towards Hargreaves. Its eyes were endless voids as it surveyed the navy-blue uniform that was decorated heavily in tiny pins, buttons and stars.

'We don't have names in the traditional formality as you do; there is no need as we all communicate via telepathy. From our birth, all important information is technologically implanted. It would be like what you call an encyclopaedia of your entire history, past and present, being placed into your brain.'

'Amazing,' said Hatfield, his blue eyes sparkling.

'This also works for every piece of knowledge our race conceives. So, by seeing one of our species whom we don't recognise in terms of rank or intelligence, the data is automatically uploaded into our consciousness. This is how we determine who is who.' The alien paused for a few seconds. Its nasal holes twitched at the strange smells that congregated within the room. 'You will have to forgive me if my speech and pronunciation seem inadequate at times,' it said as its thin lips gingerly moved, 'but we are not used to verbal communication.'

'No, you're doing absolutely fine,' interjected Hatfield as he shuffled in his crisp white laboratory jacket. 'Your grasp of the English language is exceptional.'

The alien nodded respectfully.

'Can you tell us more about this brain technology … the consciousness?'

'It is simple, Doctor. Think of your mobile phone devices, and how you access social media over your Internet.'

Hatfield grinned at the thought of the alien's knowledge of human technology. A creature from another planet talking about mobile phones and the Internet! How weird is that?

'Well,' the alien continued, 'it is the same process. Look at the Internet and the breadth of knowledge and understanding that you can benefit from, learn from. This works in a way akin to our brains. Think of it as having the Internet, and all of its worthwhile information, implanted into your head. The technology then acts as the server, allowing your eyes to view whatever you wish. This transports the required data immediately to our brains, thus we then have the knowledge of that data, and how to apply it.'

Hatfield sat astonished. 'Wow, that is incredible. So, if I wished to learn … say for example to fly an airplane, then the years of learning that it takes to accomplish this goal would be sent automatically into my brain?'

'Yes.'

'And I would instantly be an expert in flying said airplane?'

'That is correct.'

Hatfield's mouth dropped open, overwhelmed at the creature's vast intellect as he looked to Hargreaves. The General raised his eyebrows as though the admission was an everyday occurrence.

The alien sensed the fact that Hargreaves was less than impressed. It could read the way he responded, as though suspicious of how it came to know such human technologies.

It looked at the General. 'We study everything human, as no doubt you study everything alien. Don't forget, we were once at your level of being.' The alien suddenly looked away from the men. 'Who are those humans that stand over there?' it asked, distracted as it pointed a spindly index finger in the direction of the one-way mirror.

The two men turned their heads as they followed the finger from the four-digit extraterrestrial hand. 'Oh, that's just some of our more curious colleagues. You see, this is the first time that some of them have viewed an intelligent life form such as yourself. It's a monumental occasion in many of their lives,' said Hargreaves, his thoughts becoming more concerned at the alien's increasing abilities.

Thank you. Its facial skin quivered as it projected the courtesy into the General's mind.

Hargreaves' tight lips parted in a wry smile. Even extraterrestrials have a sense of humour.

'Why am I here, and what happened to my pilot?' asked the alien as it changed tack.

Hargreaves hoped that the pleasantries weren't at an end. 'You are in this facility because your ship crashed out here in the desert, three days ago. We brought you here for your own safety; after all, we didn't know at that time whether or not you could survive our atmospheric conditions. As for your pilot? I'm sorry, but he didn't survive the crash, he was too badly injured.'

Hatfield averted his eyes in respect at the alien's loss.

Its skin around its wide forehead creased as the wafer-thin eyelids dropped, narrowing its eyes. 'What have you done with the body? I would like to see the body.'

Hargreaves began fingering the small gold cuff buttons of his blazer. 'Yes, of course, but later,' he agreed, his own eyes firmly fixed on the being.

The alien looked at both of them in turn. 'I wish for the body to be left untouched. I hope this is not a problem, General, Doctor?'

Hatfield looked to the General, then back at the alien. 'I'm sorry, but you might not approve. We had to perform an autopsy to find out how it—sorry, your pilot died.' He raised his eyebrows hesitantly. 'Do you understand?'

The alien remained silent for several seconds before responding firmly. 'No experimentation.'

Hargreaves leant forward as he placed his elbows upon the desk, which creaked under the considerable weight. He stared with an air of authority at his weaker colleague, before returning his gaze back to the alien. 'Look, here on Earth we perform an autopsy on our dead. It's a way of telling whether or not they died naturally, or by any other means, you know, purposely killed.'

'If my pilot died in the crash then you know, don't you?' said the alien with caution.

Hatfield stared at the alien as beads of sweat gathered around his own flat forehead. 'Yes, but we needed to know if it was the crash or the atmosphere that killed him. As was said earlier, we didn't know at the time if your kind could survive our atmosphere.' He could instantly feel the creature trying to penetrate his mind. Either that or he was becoming increasingly paranoid. 'Anyway, your compatriot died as a result of its—his overwhelming injuries.'

The alien glared through Hatfield. 'Okay, Doctor. I understand.'

Hatfield smiled as he nodded at the alien. He felt pleased with himself at the way they both now appeared to have this mutual understanding, a kind of trust.

'So, where is my ship? Is it badly damaged?'

Hargreaves coughed as he shuffled his large body in the small frame of the chair. It looked like it was fighting a losing battle to accommodate him. 'Well, your ship was quite badly damaged. I don't think you will be going anywhere soon,' he replied with a sarcastic smile.

'Let me see it, and I shall judge for myself the extent of the damage.'

The General grimaced. 'Yes, but later.'

'General, you may as well know that your people will be unable to study the ship—I know that you have already tried. It is protected by a powerful energy field that acts as a security device if events such as these occur.' The minuscule muscles twitched slightly in its neck. 'Besides, I shall not be here for long, you do know this, don't you?'

'How so?' asked Hargreaves, his mouth and eyebrows bent downwards, puzzled.

He was beginning to enjoy the battle of wits that was now forming with the alien; the glint in his eye was obvious enough to all who watched through the one-way mirror.

'General, Doctor, I appreciate the medical care that you and your people have given me, but are you suggesting that I am a prisoner of this facility?'

Hatfield looked at the pulsating bulbous veins that held the alien's life force. He was fascinated. By squinting hard enough he could see the otherworldly blood flowing through its arms. 'No, of course not. You are a guest of this facility and the government organisation that funds it,' he said in a friendly manner, almost embarrassed by the question.

'So, I could actually get up and leave at any point if I chose to?'

Hatfield attempted a reply which turned into a bumbling stutter. He looked at the General for an intervening answer.

'Well, you could, but that wouldn't be advised,' said Hargreaves as he sensed that things were becoming uncomfortable for them all.

He sat back in the chair. His broad physique swallowed the vertical metal back rest. He ran his right hand down his face, squeezing the tired flesh. 'Look, all we would like is for you to help us answer some questions about yourself and your species. It's not every day that one comes across beings from another world. Some have waited a lifetime for just a glimpse of one such as yourself. You see, it's an extremely rare position that we are in—an extremely fortunate position at that. All we require is some insight. After that, I will personally take you to see your deceased pilot and to survey the damage to your craft.'

Hatfield watched as the alien's exterior seemed to soften, as though releasing a burst of energy.

'Okay, that seems fair, General. Ask what you may.'

The alien returned to its previous calm demeanour, all to the relief of the humans who watched.

'How do you communicate telepathically?' asked Hatfield as he thrust his youthful head forwards.

'Our brain structure is slightly different to yours. We have an over developed frontal lobe that is considerably larger than your own. This is why our cranial shell appears wider—to compensate for the expansion when used telepathically. You must know this already if you've done an "autopsy" on my pilot?' it said, turning to the General. 'If not, then ask your colleague.'

Hatfield frowned. 'I don't understand.'

Hargreaves smiled again, he knew.

The alien stared again at the General. 'There is a female human with abilities like mine, standing with your colleagues. I have felt her trying to access my brain channels since the beginning of the interview.'

Hatfield turned swiftly to the General, he required an immediate answer.

'I don't have to explain anything to you, Doctor,' said Hargreaves angrily before turning his blue eyes back towards the alien. 'Over the years we have brought in all manner of people: mediums, psychics, spiritualists—all in the real hope of understanding telepathy. But no firm conclusions were ever formed, we could never reproduce it in an ordinary human mind,' he explained, again concerned. What other information has it extracted from me?

He pulled a white papery cigarette packet from his silky inside jacket pocket. The alien watched as the General placed the small stick between his lips, and snapped open the lid of his gold coloured Zippo lighter. Its head once again tilted, startled as the flame lit one end of the stick as the human sucked on the other.

'So, telepathy is your main form of communication. What about the practice of telekinesis, can you achieve this also?' he asked, extremely interested as he blew the thick smoke from his mouth.

'Yes! Very good, General,' the alien exclaimed, the raised tone of its voice the only sign of emotion. 'Telekinesis, as you refer to it, is our main way of flying our crafts. We need a fuel type that does not exist on this planet. It is an extremely unstable combination, not unlike the elements within your nuclear fission, but even more hazardous. You see, your nuclear energy requires powerful blasts for propulsion. Also add the fact that the temperatures would be extremely hot, dangerously erratic.' It looked to the two men whom hung on its every word before continuing. 'Now, whilst we have perfected the propulsion techniques and cooling systems required for such travel, the fuel contained in our crafts makes it very difficult to negotiate great distances. This is why we use our telekinetic abilities—to control our crafts—to steady them safely as we navigate distance and travel.'

Hatfield could have sworn that he saw a flicker of excitement in the aliens' eyes as they discussed the subject. He himself certainly was excited. 'Yes, I understand that, it makes perfect sense.' He paused for a breath as an enthused, childlike smile adorned his smooth face. 'What about wormholes, are they also a part of your travel, to quicken the journey from where you came?'

'Yes, that is correct, Doctor,' replied the alien. 'Wormholes, as you call them, are an essential part of our travel. While our fuel sources are inexhaustible, they are unstable as I have previously stated. Yes, we can give stability by using our telekinetic abilities, but this we cannot do for an extended period of time—it is too dangerous for our kind.'

'Why? Why is it dangerous?'

He used his right hand to waft away the General's plume of cigarette smoke that attempted to attack his throat. Hargreaves, acknowledging that the smoke irritated his colleague, begrudgingly stubbed out the cigarette in the small round foil ashtray in front of them.

'If we use our telekinetic abilities for an extended amount of time, it causes our brains to, how would you say ... heat up, fry? They become unstable themselves, like overworked machines.'

Hargreaves leant his weary head to one side. 'Can you tell us more about these wormholes, and how they can be located, activated even?' he said as he prodded the gold Zippo lighter in the alien's direction.

'No, I'm sorry, I can't allow that,' said the alien, the answer dampening the previous enthusiasm that had built in the room.

'Why not?' asked Hatfield in a delicate manner.

'Because I was told not to.' The alien sat quietly, devoid of emotion. Its unnerving stare, cold as it looked through the humans. 'We believe that your race is still an unpredictable one, like our energy sources. Your race can't blend as one; there are so many that oppose one another still. If our technology was to be taught to you, it would be with great dread for the outcome.'

Hargreaves leant back in the chair. 'Why?'

'We have studied your planet for a Millennia, yet only a tiny speck of change has occurred; you still hate and wish to destroy one another. I fear that humanity would obliterate itself if such scientific gifts were given to you now. Besides, my superiors would be extremely unhappy if your species managed to achieve the art of interstellar travel,' it warned grimly. 'It would be disastrous to let you bring the same hatred up from the Earth and into the stars.'

'So, you are not in charge, you are not their leader?' asked Hatfield, mesmerised at how the creature's large head balanced upon its thin neck and shoulders.

The alien seemed intrigued by the question. 'You assume that I speak for my entire race... very interesting.' It seemed to ponder the question again for a brief moment. 'Would you send in your President to meet me without knowing the potential risks?'

Hatfield conceded with an agreeable nod.

'What do you know about our President?' said a perturbed Hargreaves with a frown.

'There are many who are above me in terms of authority—they will come for me soon enough.'

The two men looked at one another, disturbed by this answer.

The humans slid uncomfortably on the hard surface of the metal chairs.

'You said that you were told not to reveal certain answers to our questions, can you elaborate on this?' said Hargreaves as his eyes focused on the creature. 'I mean, are you in contact with your race now?'

'We are always in contact, General. Our form of telepathy extends far beyond the boundaries of this planet,' replied the alien.

This was what Hargreaves had feared. 'Okay, let's stay on course here,' he said, attempting to exert control. 'Why are you here? Over the last 60-70 years there have been all sorts of U.F.O. sightings and claims of abductions. Can you give us any explanations for this?'

'Yes, General. You have to understand that the universe is an immense place. Even with our technology it is still impossible to determine where the universe starts or ends, if indeed it does. What I mean is that because of this potentially infinite space it would be foolish of one—even vain—to assume that only our two species share the universe.'

The alien placed its long hands upon the desk in front of itself. It was taking all of the questions in a relaxed, almost obedient manner.

'So, species-wise, there are more than the two of us?' asked Hatfield, the childlike enthusiasm again gripping his face.

It focused its eyes upon Hargreaves. 'Ask your General, he knows this.'

The General coughed embarrassingly as he cleared his ravaged throat from years of a forty-a-day cigarette habit. 'Yes, we have documents and files on five species of extraterrestrial beings, including yourselves.'

'Five? I can assure you of around 300 separate species, including yourselves.'

Hatfield laughed as he flopped back in his chair. His mouth fell open again in astonishment as he immediately sat upright. 'Wow! Of course, we are an extraterrestrial species to you also,' he said, amazed. He tried to comb his blonde hair out of his eye line with his right hand. '300! What are the others like, are they like us?'

Hargreaves looked at the Doctor.

'Among these species there are many like us who are peaceful. There are also many who are lower than both of us in terms of evolution. Again, those who are not ready for such knowledge as it would have a devastating effect on themselves, and potentially their nearest planetary neighbours. Add to those the races what we deem as "new borns"; races in their early evolutionary years, what you might refer to as Neanderthal man. Then there are the ancient races, much older than ours. These are mainly the originals that started the Council. They are only interested in peace and prolonging their own civilisations. They have little interest in seeking out new worlds and species.'

'What about us? Are there any races similar to humans, in terms of physicality?' asked Hatfield again, his whole body eagerly hanging on the suspense as he waited for the answer.

'No, you are the only species of your kind—you are truly unique.'

Hatfield felt both deflated, yet honoured. He had always imagined an identical species living on an identical planet somewhere across the universe. Being unique, well, that he would have to settle for.

'The real fears come from the races of the Greens and Blues.'

There was suddenly an intensely quiet atmosphere as the statement sunk in.

'Greens and Blues?' said Hatfield, squinting his eyes harshly.

'Yes. The Greens and Blues are two races who are similar to us in terms of appearance—physicality as you call it—except for their skin colour. These species are incredibly hostile and dangerous. They have had many wars and disputes on many planets. Their thirst for violence goes hand in hand with their love of conflict. Fortunately, at the moment they are 200 of your Earth years behind us in terms of technology. This means that the Universal Council have some time to decide what to do about them. One day though, they will be on equal terms. This is why they love war so much, as they pillage everything from food to technological advancements from their enemy. They gain stronger with every bloody war waged. They—'

'Wait,' said Hatfield, holding up his right hand to interrupt. 'When you say 200 Earth years behind us in terms of technology, do you mean behind you, or us humans?' He had loved the possibility of this. The alien races that caused mayhem in the many science-fiction movies he had watched as a child exhilarated him. Now though, he sat stone-faced at the real fact that this could happen one day. He ran his tongue over his teeth as he thought for a few seconds. 'If these races are as dangerous as you suggest, then why doesn't your "Council" destroy them?'

'The Council have always believed in a universal peace. We have encountered previous races with grand designs of war, but things have always been resolved. You see, the Council consists of a member of every known race throughout the universe, selected on a strict criteria, peace being the predominant attribute.'

The alien turned once again to Hargreaves. 'I apologise. To answer your first question, General, yes ... we are responsible for many abductions, though these are for scientific purposes only. We have never harmed any race that we have taken for such curiosities. My main point in expanding on the numerous races in the universe was to show that my species is not responsible for every abduction, mutilated animal or sighting. Don't forget other races are just as curious, some more so.'

Hargreaves nodded his head as he thought about this. 'Do you mean that this "Universal Council" is some sort of planetary guardian?' he asked, trying to understand the concept.

'As I explained before, there are members of a Council—like the governments of your world—who decide, and act for the good of the universe,' replied the alien.

It placed its index finger into the foil ashtray and touched the crumbling ash. It moved its digit towards the tiny nose holes that sat flush upon its oval face. Curiously, it sniffed gently at its finger; its lips curled at the displeasure of the smell. Hargreaves smiled, amused at the effect.

'So, what would happen if these "Greens and Blues" ever invaded our planet? Would our current technology be able to defend such an invasion?'

'No, General,' said the alien sadly. 'I'm afraid that the end result would be the entire annihilation of your complete species.'

'How long would we have before these invaders would be upon this planet, or even in our atmosphere?' Hargreaves continued, obviously interested on a military scale.

'I've said enough for now. I've said too much.'

The alien sat in eerie silence as though in a trance. It stared again at the colourful pins that were lined in formation across the General's left breast of his blue blazer.

They all sat for a few minutes before Hargreaves pushed back his metal chair; the scraping noise made the alien purse its thin lips.

He stood and straightened his clothing. 'I'll be back in a couple of minutes, I need some air,' he said, swiftly heading out of the door.

The alien watched in stillness. It could sense that something was wrong. Human emotions offer such bizarre facial expressions, which often betray their real thoughts.

Hatfield also sat quietly. He felt lost, cautious as both he and the alien gazed at each other. The more he focused on the humanoid's eyes, the more he felt like he was being hypnotised. He smiled awkwardly, then grimaced as he realised that the facial gesture would probably have no meaning to the alien, or so he thought.

Hargreaves returned after several minutes. He entered the room with an overweight dark-haired woman, in her mid-forties. He offered his chair to her as he took a step backwards. Hatfield shot the General an icy look so as to ask what was going on.

The alien immediately knew who the woman was.

'Why have you brought one of your "mediums" with you?' it said as it surveyed her large frame.

Hargreaves nodded towards the woman, who then turned and faced the alien. Her small hazel eyes lie mostly hidden beneath the bangs of her shoulder length bob. They appeared set back, deep within the sockets as her hair framed her chubby face harshly. She focused on the creature before her; the intensity was intimidating, even for the strongest of men.

'Why is she attempting to read my mind, and who is Harry White, the Sec Def? said the alien. 'What does it mean?'

'I'm sorry, but we need to know more about what you're not telling us. I didn't want to do this, but you haven't given us much choice,' replied Hargreaves.

Hatfield turned to the General. 'Can I talk to you for a minute?' He followed Hargreaves out of the door and stood behind the mirror, away from the other personnel. 'What the hell are you doing, General? This wasn't part of the agenda!' he said angrily.

'Look, I haven't got time for this. Doctor, we need to know the truth. What if these Greens and Blues are really only a handful of years from getting here?' Hargreaves pushed his square face into the Doctor's own. 'Wouldn't you want to know, so you could gain a possible advantage?'

'Yes of course, b—but—' stuttered Hatfield.

'But nothing! It even said itself that it had told us too much. It's hiding something and my superiors want to know what, that's why they've sent her in with me.' Hargreaves looked through the translucent mirror, pointing towards the medium's rotund back sitting upright in the chair. 'I still have to take orders, Doctor, as do you.'

The alien looked towards the one-way mirror as it held its mind closed to the medium's prying interference. 'She is very strong. I am intrigued as to why you haven't cracked telepathy yet.'

Hargreaves gestured for an angry Hatfield to quieten down as the words echoed around the walls. The General returned his attention towards the room. What makes you think that we haven't cracked telepathy?

The Doctor wasn't happy as he joined his colleagues at the glass. They all gazed through its thickness back into the room. Two shadowy movements were all that could be seen within the darkness, silent as they became locked in a battle of the minds, focusing all of their energies on blocking one another's intrusions.

'I don't like this, General. We've completely destroyed any trust that we had built with it.'

'Duly noted, Doctor. Now quit your whining, we might yet need you.'

'Need me for what?' whispered Hatfield in a discontented grumble.

Hargreaves turned his attention back to the Doctor. 'Remember when it said that their telekinetic abilities only lasted for so long? Well, things could get messy.'

Hatfield shook his head as he spoke. 'You're hoping that it's going to try to break out using its abilities, aren't you?'

'You're catching on, Doctor,' said Hargreaves, an aggressive sneer crossing his red face. 'That's why the medium is in there, to try to keep it grounded with her own abilities, as well as endeavouring to extract the relevant information.' He looked back through the glass. 'Eventually, as it said before, it'll end up frying—but not before I get the truth.'

Hatfield closed his eyes tight, again shaking his head in fury. It was no use arguing, he couldn't win.

'We've been here for what… one hour and forty-seven minutes,' sighed Hatfield as he tapped the plastic face of his digital watch.

'Look!' exclaimed the young ginger-haired female colleague who stood with them.

They all turned their attention back towards the mirror. The alien's rangy arms had dropped to its side; its spider-like hands brushed the ruby red carpeted floor as it began to wilt. The black eyes had lost their darkness and were now beginning to turn a milky light brown colour. Its body began slipping down the back of the metal chair as a slight rasp exhaled from its lips.

'For God's sake, General,' shouted Hatfield, begging for the torture to end, 'you're killing it!'

'Almost there, Doctor. Get ready to go in.'

The table began to levitate slowly in the middle of the room. The camera tilted downwards on its tripod as its steel hollow legs began to bend and buckle. A brown liquid started to trickle from the alien's nasal holes. The medium's head now began to shake violently as blood started to stream from her nose and ears. Her eyes—bloodshot from the minuscule blood vessels that were bursting simultaneously—became covered in a thin red film.

Hatfield attempted to get to the door, but was forcibly restrained by Hargreaves; the Doctor's strength was no match against the stronger, bigger man's. 'What the hell are you playing at?' He winced as the General's hold tightened around his slight upper arm. The increasing pressure was too much as he tried to prise the fingers open.

'Not yet, Doctor.'

An ear-piercing screech flew from the mouth of the alien. The medium collapsed from the chair, falling to the floor with a dense thud. The table fell from the air, crashing between them as the two minds lost their fixed concentration. The camera fell sideways, causing several small black pieces to break off and scatter across the carpet. Its light petered to a dull red before fading completely.

'GO, GO!' shouted Hargreaves as he pushed Hatfield forward, eager to get him into the room to save both human and alien lives.

Hatfield leapt to the aid of the creature, cradling its large head as he froze, unable to think straight, what to do. Hargreaves leant down towards the medium as other doctors from the compound raced to offer medical assistance. He stared into the red, wide open eyes of the bleeding woman.

He gripped her broad shoulders with his rough hands, and hauled her heavy build up. 'What did you get, what did you get?' he repeated urgently as he wiped the blood from her full mouth.

'They have—they have been studying us for—for years, since time began,' she sputtered, gurgling on the excess blood. 'We are their—their experiment, they are our Gods, our creators! They bred us—'

She became cut off as the Doctors battled to save her life.

'For what? Bred us for what?' raged Hargreaves as his spittle dotted her cold swollen face.

'They bred us for war, their army—for war against—'

Hargreaves began shaking the dying woman. 'Against who? Tell me!'

He sensed that the medium was close to death. Her eyes rolled into the back of her round head as more claret liquid ran from her thick nose.

'We're going to have to move her, and quickly,' said one of the Doctors with urgency as a gurney burst into the room.

The medium clasped the General's hand. 'They bred us for war—for war against the Greens and Blues,' she whispered in a cracked breath before releasing her hold.

Despite his age, Hargreaves moved spritely towards the alien. The milky brown substance was running from its eyes, spilling all over Hatfield's trembling hands.

The General knelt down beside the distressed young Doctor. 'When are they coming? You tell me when they are coming, goddamn it!'

The aliens' lips quivered slightly as it tried to speak. Hatfield looked to Hargreaves before lowering his right ear towards its slit-like mouth.

'Pathetic humans—anything believe. We are—already. Here, we are—already here.'

The broken words entered the doctor's head as the alien used the last of its strength. A final musty breath blew softly from its mouth. Its thin leathery chest slowly deflated as the remaining air exited the body. Wrinkles adorned the dry withered flesh as its arms fell back to the floor.

Hatfield lowered the alien's head gently to the soft floor. A look of heartfelt sadness washed over his face.

Hargreaves gripped Hatfield's collar with a firm left hand. 'Well?' he asked aggressively, his eyes wild as he demanded an immediate answer. 'What did it say?'

Hatfield turned to the General, slowly wiping the sweat from his forehead with the sleeve of his right forearm. 'It's all lies... it's nothing but a game to them,' he said nervously with a pale, blank expression on his face. 'They're already here.'

Chapter 7

We Don't Know

Something caught Mark's eye. He turned his head towards the door, staring hard as he began crawling on all fours across the room.

'What are you doing, Mark?' John asked with a deep sigh.

The Professor could feel the wetness of the General's blood clinging to his hands and knees; the liquid dampened his trousers, spreading like a fungus as it soaked itself deeper into the denim fabric.

A glimmer spiked the mist as he approached. 'What is that?'

'What is it?' said John as he trailed the direction of Mark's voice. 'What have you seen?'

'I don't know.' Mark fumbled around the floor before placing his hands on a solid metallic object. 'Gotcha!' He quietly slipped the cylindrical shape into his back pocket, and made his way over to the wall. 'Look what I've got,' he said as the others closed either side of him. He carefully pulled the gadget from his pocket, flashing it quickly.

'What the hell is it?' said John again, his interest heightened as he looked around the room with a sheepish nervousness.

'I think it's one of their weapons. They must have dropped it during the struggle,' replied Mark.

'That's great. I hate to put a downer on things, but what can we do against them with one weapon?'

James extended his fingers and ran them over the object's metal surface. 'It's a start, John. We have a little leverage here. We might be able to at least kill one of these fuckers, eh?'

'Exactly. There could be a number of ways in which we could use this,' grinned Mark as he stared at them in turn.

John pushed his head forwards. 'How?'

'Let me stew on this for a while, I'll see what I can come up with.'

'Yeah, well don't burn the stew, Professor,' rambled John with a serious look upon his heavy face, 'we might not have much longer left to eat it.'

The three of them sat in the grease and dirt, silent. The hunger and tiredness was beginning to really hit them hard.

John's stomach grumbled loudly, the sound pulling the other two from a drifting half sleep. 'I don't feel too good, I'm starting to feel faint,' he said as he held his abdomen, trying to suppress the angry noise.

Mark opened his eyes, startled at the intrusion before the words sunk in. 'Ride it out, John.' He sat upright against the wall, exhausted. 'This is what happens when you don't get your nutrients. Without hydration we're all doomed, this is what the General was getting at,' he said, himself starting to feel similar effects.

'I'm not pissing and drinking it! I want some self-respect to remain at least.'

'I think the time for self-respect disappeared long ago. If you want to last longer, then you're going to have to bite the bullet—we all are.'

James threw his arms up. 'Anyway, forget about that,' he said, now fully awake. 'What the fuck are we going to do? We have a weapon here, we need to use it.'

'Keep your voice down!' whispered Mark as he looked around. 'This is our only advantage, and I would like it to stay that way.'

'Then we need to use it. You keep talking about hydration and drinking piss, yet by the time we get around to doing anything we'll all be bloody dead!'

Mark tutted. 'James, haven't you learnt anything?' he said, sighing as he looked to the ceiling light. 'Look at what has happened so far, it hasn't panned out too well has it.'

'What's the point, the outcome is inevitable,' added John, frustrated. 'Why are we prolonging things?'

The Professor shook his head. 'If the whole world turned around and gave in to every situation in life, then the human race would have died out thousands of years ago.' He yawned as he spoke. 'This is why they're testing us constantly, to break us down, to see what we are, to see what makes us, well... us.'

'I don't buy it,' sneered John. 'Besides, we have no idea how long they've been watching our planet.' He wiped the drool from the corner of his mouth with his jacket sleeve. 'Look at all these TV programmes. According to them, aliens have been scouring our planet for years, centuries even! Who knows, maybe we're their experiment, and they're our makers?!'

'Jesus fucking Christ, will the pair of you stop talking shit, you're doing my head in!' shouted James as he rose to his feet. 'Give me that weapon, I'll blast those gangly fucks!'

He moved to grab the device from the Professor's hand.

Mark pulled his arm back. 'Superb, the whole ship will come running then!'

'Well it's better than sitting here listening to you two talk crap!'

Mark pondered the last two statements for a second. 'Actually, that might not be a bad idea.'

'What? What idea?'

'If the worst comes to the worst, we could destroy as much of the circuitry and lighting in here as possible.

'To gain what?' interrupted John. 'What good would that do us?'

'Put it this way, they would certainly come running. You never know, with this weapon we could take the whole ship down.'

'How and why would we want to do that?' said James.

Mark now climbed to his feet and stared through the haze towards James. 'What's around the corners of the corridor?'

James rolled his eyes sarcastically. 'I don't know.'

'Exactly—we don't know.' Mark pointed at the two men. 'We could be close to a control room, another prison. Hell, there could be many more of us here somewhere, we don't know.'

'That's right, we don't know!' replied James with a smile to suggest that the Professor was reaching.

'Think about it. What if at the end of the corridor there were hundreds more rooms like this, thousands? There might be as many humans in as many rooms.'

'Yeah, and your point is, Professor?'

'If we could free enough of them, then we might be able to overrun these bloody things.'

James puffed out his cheeks in disappointment. 'I'm surprised at you, Mark. I think that you need to drink some urine, the dehydration is clearly affecting your brain!'

John managed a sputtered laugh. 'I'm sorry,' he said.

'Now you're cracking jokes. What have you done since we arrived, eh?' asked Mark, obviously annoyed at the mocking. 'I'm telling you, there are others here. I heard cries earlier, especially when Daniel made a break for it.'

James growled in frustration as he turned away from Mark. 'Please. Say, for example, there are others here, what are you going to do, create an army?' He turned back and faced the Professor. 'Six of us couldn't defeat two or three of those bastards, so how the fuck do you expect an army to beat them?' He paused for a moment to calm himself. 'You don't think that there're only a few creatures on this ship, do you?'

'Of course not! But again we don't know how big this craft is, or where we are.'

'Bingo, Professor. Give the man a prize—that's the point!' James clapped his hands in derision. 'Think about what you're saying. It's suicide, and that's before we've even got to the end of the corridor.'

Mark dropped to the floor, his legs stretched out in front of him as he sat. 'I'm sorry, I don't know what's happening to me. My thought... my rational thought is jumbled all over the place.'

'It's alright, Mark.' James planted a hand upon the Professor's left shoulder. 'You said it yourself, it's a lack of nutrients. Add to this no food, sleep, warmth—it's shutting us down, either that or it's this damn mist,' he said, waving his right hand through the red tinge.

'I did wonder that myself,' said Mark as he raised his head. 'I still believe that it's what kept us knocked out. I'd like to know the chemical compound of it, to know if it's toxic or not.'

'In fact, do you think this is what's depleting us, weakening us?' John asked as he moved in front of the two men.

'No, I think you will find that this is good old-fashioned basics. As James said, it's just our bodies starting to shut down due to our needs.'

John scratched the back of his head. 'But why is this mist here, what's its purpose?'

Mark shrugged. 'It's bizarre. If it's nothing to do with our unconsciousness then it could just be that it's an emission of some type, you know, like a car emitting smoke and fumes from its exhaust.' He rubbed his hands together to warm them. 'Could be the same principle, and we're just unlucky to have been slung in here with it.'

James' mouth curled downwards as his eyebrows raised, pondering the thoughts. 'Well, it would make sense to a degree. But then why would the emissions be here in this room, and not flowing out into the atmosphere from an "alien" exhaust pipe?'

'I don't know,' wondered Mark. 'We haven't conquered space or its long-term travel yet. We've only scratched the surface of what is possible. There could be a thousand reasons why.'

'Yes, I know,' replied James as he looked around again, 'we're only speculating.'

'Absolutely, I agree. It's only speculation, but it doesn't hurt to try and have some understanding of what we are dealing with. The more we know, the better the chance there is of doing something.'

'Of course, you're right.' James tip-toed to his full height. His head pushed aside a layer of the mist; it swirled around his head like clouds atop a mountain peak as he reached upwards. 'Maybe it's like emissions, from emissions?'

'That's interesting, but the ventilations are there, trust me. If it is emissions leftovers, you still need ventilation for the waste to waft through into this room,' said Mark. 'If they weren't, then the whole room would be swamped in the stuff.'

'Yeah, but it is,' frowned John.

'No, I mean really flooded in the stuff, like being trapped in a burning building; the thickness that blinds you, the toxins that choke you—that level of smoke, or in this case, mist.' Mark grimaced as he scratched his head. 'Even though the visibility in here isn't great, there is still a degree of it, we can just about see. No, the more I think about it the more it makes sense—we are where we're meant to be.'

James rubbed his stubbled chin. 'Okay, how do you know for sure?'

'For a start there is breathable oxygen in here—if there wasn't then we would be dead. Add to this the fact that if these are smoke or fumes from an emission, then without some form of ventilation we would have suffered from the effects hours ago.'

'Yes, but if they're much more technologically advanced, then isn't it also possible that they would have solved these problems? Would they not know how to disperse dangerous toxins from their own ships, or to convert these toxins into harmless emissions, if what we are talking about is indeed the cause.' James rubbed hard at the back of his slim neck, it ached. 'And what if the aliens have the same, or a similar respiratory system to what we have? Surely it would affect them in an identical way if they breathe the same air as us?'

'Hmmm, I hadn't considered that,' replied Mark, thinking on the questions. He now began rubbing the back of his own neck. 'It is possible. Just because they come from a different planet it doesn't necessarily mean that they have a different atmosphere to ours. This could be why they are interested in Earth.'

'Now that definitely makes sense,' said John, pointing at the Professor.

Mark shook his head as he looked to each of them. 'Again, most of this is guess work. If these intelligences are far more advanced, then I imagine that they would be powering their crafts by some form of nuclear power. It depends where they come from and how their chemical elements differ from ours. Though I imagine that their intelligence would allow them the freedoms to devise many different types of reactors capable of producing various energy sources.'

'Think about it,' said James as he smiled. 'The aliens have strutted up and down the corridor and in and out of the room since we woke. They either breath the same air as we do, or the mist is only harmful to us.'

'You're right,' yielded Mark, 'it's that simple.' A curious look spread over the Professor's face. 'How do you know all of this stuff anyway, and why didn't you speak up earlier?'

James stared at the Professor, as much baffled by the question as he was the answer. 'I don't know, bits and pieces. Like you said, fragments come and go.'

James awoke with a start as the nightmare threatened his light sleep. He looked around, still dazed before his vision cleared slightly. Flesh, urine, faeces and sweat—the odour clung to the air like a putrid disease. He winced at the stench as he cupped his oily face, massaging the skin firmly as he sought to loosen the tension in his muscles.

'You okay?' asked John. He too had been dozing lightly.

James looked at the equally exhausted man. 'Yeah, where's Mark?'

John looked around, waving the mist out of his eye-line. 'Mark,' he called out in a deep voice.

The tin-like sound of liquid trickled against metal, echoing off the walls around them followed by a gagging, retching noise.

'Mark?' called John again, concerned.

'I'm okay,' he said as he came through the haze, fiddling with the button fly of his jeans. 'It's quite difficult to urinate, catch it, and then drink it at the same time!'

John looked at James; they both simultaneously pulled the same screwed up face in disgust. 'Each to their own,' said John at the thought.

Suddenly, the glow from the triangular panel burst through the smoky atmosphere. The three men each closed their eyes as they shuffled their bodies out of reach of the luminescence.

Two Greys appeared to hover as they entered the stench-ridden box. Their deep eyes scanned the room menacingly as they hunted the humans. The men crouched within the mist, crawling from side to side as alien feet clattered closer.

'The weapon, Mark,' whispered James loudly, 'use the weapon!'

John scrambled into view, desperate to evade the hunters. Mark could see the man's gritted teeth as his face searched the room. The haze circled around John's frightened features, teasing them cruelly as beads of sweat dropped from his thick, anguished face.

Mark gently moved his hand around to his back pocket and pulled out the small tubular gadget. His hand trembled as he held the metallic object out in front of him. His heart skipped a beat, causing him to nearly drop it as James' shoulder collided with his own.

'Fuck,' said James as he gripped Mark's left forearm with his right hand.

John's head came hurtling through the haze, breaking its curling rhythm. The same clenched teeth and wrinkled expression accompanied it. 'Christ, th-th-there you are!' he stammered, fear coursing through his body.

James gestured frantically for John to join them, to become a single unit. John smiled, relieved as he made his way towards them. Without warning, his scampering body stopped in its tracks. The blood drained from his face, changing into one of white horror.

'Come on,' begged James, extending his arm out to help.

John's head plummeted to the floor, exploding like a melon as it slammed into the grating. The others watched as the creature lifted John's mangled head. Blood poured from his mouth, followed by several broken teeth that floated over the red surface. They slid over his glistening lips, and down his chin. His nose lay bent across the side of his right cheek, as parts of bone protruded through what was left of the skin. His meaty tongue—bitten almost clean through—hung by a stringy thread before its weight forced it to the grating with a wet slap. His legs kicked out with an instinctive reflex, as though desperate for someone to grasp them as he began sliding backwards, and out of view.

Mark and James tightened their hold on one another. 'I'm sorry,' muttered Mark under his breath. They looked to the floor, both ashamed yet scared in equal measure.

A tall thin silhouette remained; it stood quiet, still. Its head turned upon its bony shoulders as it scanned the room. With lightning speed it dropped through the mist onto all four limbs, and began prowling forwards like an animal preparing to strike. The two men instinctively leapt backwards. With nowhere to go, their heads smashed against the wall as the creature's face intruded upon their space. They could feel its slimy skin as they trembled, forehead to forehead; its nostrils quivered as it drank in their human scent.

Mark's fingers desperately pushed every button and switch on the device. A loud crackle snapped in the air as green streams of electrical charge fizzled, lighting up the mist that tried to smother it. He rammed the weapon into the alien's skeletal neck; its face contorted—grimacing with pain as it clamped its vein-covered eyelids shut.

James clasped Mark's arms, adding extra strength and leverage behind the weapon as they forced it deeper into the creature's neck. It parted its lips as the power surged through its body. The colourful charge glowed through its thin skin, flickering as it shot to the roof of its small mouth.

Mark used all of his remaining strength, almost breaking his fingers as he forced the buttons down on the weapon. The alien shook violently as its flesh began to sizzle and burn. In a desperate last effort it crashed its arm down upon the device, causing the men to break their grasp. The weapon skidded across the grating, hitting the wall. The alien fell backwards, clawing at the grease before climbing awkwardly to its feet. It regained its bearings and staggered out of the room.

The door zipped shut behind it. The men breathed a sigh of relief, all the while digging their nails into each other's flesh.

'Oh fuck, my God,' panted James as he tried to collect himself. 'It's alright, its gone.'

'I think we pissed it off,' replied Mark as he sat shaking uncontrollably. 'But trust me, it'll be back sooner rather than later.' He extended his legs outwards. 'Jesus!' he cried. The outer rubber of the soles of his boots squeaked as John's blood began to soak into the suede-like material. He kicked out repeatedly as he tried to cover the red that was beginning to stain; he scraped the sides of his boots in the grease and dirt, desperate to hide the widening marks.

James slid down the wall next to the Professor. 'Fuck!' he shouted as he rammed his fists against the floor.

'This isn't happening,' said Mark. He struggled to calm himself from the encounter. His terror turned into nausea as he noticed John's pink fleshy tongue sitting in the grime, staring back at him. He kicked out furiously. 'Fuck off!' It took several attempts before he finally connected with it, sending the lump hurtling further into the mist and out of sight. He covered his face with the palms of his clammy hands as the tears started to run. 'The look... The look on his face, he was petrified,' he sniffled.

'I know, mate,' said James. He stared in despair at the Professor. 'We need to stay calm. I need you here with me.'

Chapter 8

The Angelic Deceit—John's Story

An icy breeze whistled over the iron and concrete structure of London Bridge. Cars sped across, ignorant of each other on their single-minded journeys. The towers speared the night sky from afar as small snowflakes fell delicately from above.

John Chapman shivered uncontrollably as he tiptoed over the thick broken glass. He negotiated his way through the white criss-cross window frames. Once through, he stood upright upon the blue metal edging, in between the towers' two high walkways. The wind ripped through the dark hair that framed his 39-year-old round face. He scowled uncomfortably at the effort. His hands were white, numb as they gripped the frames; he tried to steady his slightly overweight build.

His olive parka jacket draped heavily behind him. The navy denim jeans he wore clung to his already frozen legs, the wetness stinging them. He stood upon the icy ledge, sobbing hysterically as he slid his broken soul along its slippery surface. His right arm hooked the steel pillar that sat at the left, north west tower end, holding him in position as his brown eyes gazed out across the Thames; the water looked back at him—black, bleak. His open jacket invited in the wintry breeze as the chill circulated his body. He sighed wearily. A heavy trail of breath flowed from his purple lips. He could taste the salty tears that raced each other down the sides of his face; they hung at the corners of his mouth before trickling along his chapped lips. He shuffled along the ledge inch by inch, slipping twice on the frosty steel.

'No, not yet,' he said in a quiet, jittery voice. 'I'm going to try and do this right.'

'Why are you doing this, John?' asked a loud voice that rose above the thunderous sounds of the traffic below.

John slipped again, startled by the sudden intrusion as he looked downwards at his footing. 'What—what do you want?' he said aggressively as he tried to balance himself like a circus high wire act. 'Leave me alone.'

He regained his composure as he turned his head up towards the voice. He narrowed his eyes in the disorientating snow. His hair—glued to his face—became intolerable as he struggled to peer through its matted wetness. A white glow began growing, expanding eerily from the top of the walkway. He raised his left hand, attempting to shield his eyes from the blinding light. Spreading his fingers, he stared through them, frowning as the glimmering ball grew into the silhouette of a man. He almost lost his grip again as his eyes struggled to focus. His breathing increased rapidly, he couldn't work out if he was delirious or not. The light faded out to reveal a shadow, which began climbing down from the roof of the walkway. This unsettled him more.

'Stay back!' he threatened, 'I'll do it, I'll jump... I will!'

The stranger leapt effortlessly onto the ledge next to him, forcing him to grip the giant steel pillar with two hands as he clung on.

'Hi, I'm Michael. You might know me better as the archangel Michael?' said the tall, handsome man.

John's eyes widened as Michael began tiptoeing sprightly upon the ledge, like a pirouetting ballerina in jest. 'Who the hell are you?' he asked, his face pressed hard against the thick cold steel. 'And how did you do that?' He looked around, puzzled as he wondered why the stranger was there with him. 'Where did you come from?'

'I told you, I am Michael.' The dark curly-haired archangel moved closer towards John. His three-quarter length black woollen jacket whipped through the thin air as he edged along the frosty ledge. The pleated black trousers that he wore flapped in the breeze, like pantaloons from a long forgotten era. Piercing blue eyes penetrated John's ravaged soul. 'So, I understand that you wish to die?' he said jovially as the wind pushed his generous mop of hair back from his wide forehead.

'Who are you, how can you do that?' said John again, as his eyes travelled the length of Michael's athletic frame.

'Are you deaf? I'm Michael. Now come, you wish to die, do you not?'

With that, Michael grabbed John by his left upper arm, and leapt off the ledge.

'No, no, no!' screamed John as he tried to resist before losing his footing.

Several seconds had passed before John came to his senses. There, ten feet away from the paint-flaked blue ledge, the two of them hovered in midair. He turned frantically as he struggled to comprehend what was really happening. His fear multiplied as he stared at Michael. Two white feathery wings—each eight-feet in length—slowly beat amidst the wind and snow. John let out a painful cry as the grip tightened upon both his upper arms.

Michael cocked his head to one side and smiled. 'Do you still wish to die, hesitant one?' He flashed a seductive pearly white grin. He could feel the fear race through the human's body. 'Let me give you the choice.'

This failed to reassure his human cousin. They flew underneath the walkway, emerging on the opposite side. John wriggled, panicking over the bizarre situation. His heart felt like it was going to explode through his chest. He felt nauseous as he looked down at the dark, unwelcoming water.

Michael leant his head towards John's wind-battered ear. His warm lips gently grazed John's chilled skin. 'Has your longing for death deserted you?'

'Put me back, put me back!' cried John as his feet danced, desperately seeking solid ground.

Michael shook his head, disappointed at having to deal with yet another potential waste of mortal life. He floated back under the walkway and towards the inside ledge. He let go of John's arms, smiling as the human dropped onto the white criss-cross structure.

'Christ!' said John loudly as he hung on for life, shaking as he watched the archangel casually walk the edging.

Michael's wings folded behind him, hidden like they were never there. He purposefully flicked out his jacket from his sides. He sat upon the thin ledge and leant back against the structure. He tapped the hollow metal, gesturing for John to sit next to him.

Still badly shaken, John gingerly inched towards the archangel. His wet clothes hindered the effort as he lowered his feet onto the ledge next to the celestial being. His frozen face stared at Michael's warmth.

'What are you doing here, and where did you come from?' he said again softly, calmly. 'Are you… are you an angel?'

Michael's eyes pleaded to the Heavens for common sense to prevail. 'What is it with you humans? You've seen two feathered wings, yet still you question me! I've told you, I'm an archangel,' he replied in an exasperated tone. He looked directly into John's wind-stung eyes. 'Yes. My Lord has sent me down to you in your hour of need. He is sad that you humans seem to suffer so, to feel the need to leave mortality so frequently.'

John turned his head away from Michael, feeling bemused, and a little embarrassed.

'Look, why are we really here, John?' sighed Michael, realising that he may have been a little too harsh.

John began to weep. 'I can't take anymore. I've no job, and my wife is sleeping with another man! My children hate me as they blame me for the things I can't give them. I take out loans to provide for them, yet they brand me a loser when the bailiffs come calling.' John dropped his head in shame.

Michael subtly shook his head, rolling his eyes at what he deemed "trivial" matters. 'These are simple things that can be corrected, John,' he said. 'Go get a job. Find a new wife. Clear your debts and discipline your children on the rights and wrongs of your financial burdens.'

Watery drops fell from John's wet hair as his empty eyes turned to Michael's unearthly ones, which glowed through the darkness; he noticed for the first time how bright they actually were.

'Do you honestly think that if things were that simple I would be sitting here now?' asked John, amazed at Michael's seeming lack of understanding. 'You wouldn't understand—you're not human.'

'No, I'm not, thank the Lord!' exclaimed Michael as he looked to the skies, his arms held in mock prayer. 'Look down below. Look at all the hustle and traffic as everyone goes about their business. Do you think that you are the only one who has such problems?'

John glanced down and surveyed the traffic for a moment. Tiny yellow dotted headlights raced left and right as they burst through the slight mist.

Michael suddenly pointed to a black BMW convertible that sped through the traffic. 'There!' he said aloud. 'See that driver there? He has it all. He has the model looks, the cars, the house and the trophy wife… the whole package. Is he happy? No.'

'Well, he's greedy then. I would kill for that life,' said John with a jealous sneer.

'Many probably would, John.' Michael looked to the human and waited a few seconds before continuing. 'But what his wife doesn't know is that he has cancer, and they are penniless. All of his treatments cost thousands of pounds, for which he has been stealing the money from his IT company. He daren't tell his wife as he wishes to keep her in the lifestyle that she is accustomed to. What he doesn't realise though is that if he was honest with her, then she would give up everything material as long as he survives.' He stared at the human's reaction before they both watched solemnly as the BMW roared into the distance.

'So he dies?' asked John in a cracked voice. 'How do you know all of this?'

Water droplets flicked through the air as Michael ruffled his black mane. 'My Lord knows all, that is why I have been sent. But I only know these things once I am here on Earth.' Michael paused again before entertaining a simpler example. 'Think of a patients' file that one would receive from a doctor's surgery. It's sort of like a mental projection of that.'

'But does he die?' asked John again, pushing the question.

'I can't answer that. It all depends on whether the angel assigned to him can appeal to his soul or not.' He looked hard into John's eyes. 'And how badly he wants to be saved.'

Michael gazed sadly at the moving sea of light below him. The traffic reminded him of lonely ships, lost in a murky ocean, floating aimlessly before crashing into the rocks of life.

The wind howled across the walkway. John struggled to protect his eyes from the now blizzard-like conditions. He pulled the jacket hood over his aching head; flakes of ice stuck to the faux-fur trim, a wetness spreading as they melted. He turned to the archangel, his eyes peering from underneath the fur.

Michael's legs dangled over the ledge, swinging in a childlike motion. The loose, sodden laces of his black boots swayed from side to side like feeble pendulums. He cast his eyes out past the second walkway towards the water that rippled gently, as though itself shivering from the cold.

'Do you read the Bible, John?'

John paused for thought. 'No, well, some parts maybe. I was taught some stuff in school.'

'What sort of stuff?' came the slightly offended reply.

'Stuff, you know, the old classics as I call them,' he said with a shrug of his shoulders. 'Like David and Goliath, Daniel and the lions, stories like that.' John's enthusiasm suddenly increased rapidly. 'Did these things really happen? There must have been angels who witnessed these "events". I mean, you must know, right?'

Michael smiled. 'Yes, these stories are real, although not always in the context or the extremity as one reads in the Bible. Time has unfortunately turned the wonders of the Lord and his miracles into a shameful business. Did you know that religion is in the top three most profitable businesses in the world? Disgusting.' More droplets of water flew from him as he shook his head angrily. 'To answer your question though, time has distorted these events. Yes, David took on Goliath, but that wasn't how it was portrayed in the Bible. Do you know what it was?' he laughed. 'It was a simple fist fight, that's all!' Michael's body shook as he chuckled again. 'Goliath was big, but a boxing match with a lucky punch nevertheless, as you might call such a thing.'

John raised his eyebrows at the admission. 'Are all of the events like this—exaggerated?'

'Pretty much,' nodded Michael, his mouth curling downwards in frustration.

'What about you, Michael. Is your story real?'

Michael turned to John sharply. His wind swept hair blew sideways as he squinted. 'You'd better believe it!' he said, his eyes wide. 'I led my Lord's army of angels against our fallen brother, Lucifer. Gabriel and Raphael were my right and left wing lieutenants, and together we defeated the armies of darkness. I killed Lucifer myself and ended a Millenia of war!'

Michael leapt to his feet from the ledge. He proceeded to gesticulate how he won the war, re-enacting the final moments—how he placed his foot upon Lucifer's neck, and plunged his holy sword into the enemy's heart.

John sat watching stoney-faced. He wrapped his arms around his shivering rain-soaked body, fighting to keep warm.

The two sat there quietly for a while. Traffic provided the only sounds as they stared down at the world below them.

'How many angels are in Heaven?' John, broke their silence, intrigued.

His eyes surveyed the dripping feathery wings which had reappeared; they now offered him some protection from the continuous cold blasts.

'There are thousands of us,' said Michael. 'Though not all angels are like me.'

John narrowed his eyes as the bitter breeze stung them. 'I don't get it, what do you mean?'

Michael exhaled a lazy breath. 'Look, there are nine choirs of angels. You have three sets of three, each set containing three choirs. The top choirs are the Seraphim, Cherubim and the Thrones, these are the closest to God, the ones who are constantly within his presence. Next are the Dominions, Virtues and Powers, the middle ones as it were. And finally the Principalities, Archangels and Angels.'

John turned to Michael and laughed. 'You mean to say that you're in the bottom tier, second from last?' He was both amused and miffed at the thought. 'You, the slayer of Lucifer! How can this be?'

The archangel sighed with frustration. He began walking the ledge with his hands in his pockets as he tutted. 'I know, tell me about it! I'm loved in Heaven for ending the war, yet here I am helping humans on this God-forsaken rock!'

'You can't tell me that you haven't been rewarded for all that you've done in Heaven, can you?' chuckled John in a disbelieving tone.

'The only reward we seek is the reward of love from our Lord Almighty. Humans, not all, but most, thrive on the power and riches of your world. Most would do anything at any cost to succeed, to climb the ladder as it were. Don't get me wrong, I can understand the end game for their logic. Most seek only the means to survive, to give their families a better life. But if only they knew of the love, the paradise and the peace that awaits them in Heaven. If they knew, they would think and act differently, of that I am certain.'

John pursed his lips. 'Michael, that's impossible as no human can see Heaven. Don't you think that if we could, then the world would run differently, perhaps perfectly?'

Michael clasped his soft hands together. 'And that's the point!' he said smiling as he looked at John's frozen face. 'It's called faith, John. It's all about faith.'

The snow had turned more into sleet, even though the temperature had remained the same.

'What about people like me?' asked John, his teeth chattering.

Michael appeared perplexed by the question. 'What about you?'

'Well, if I had jumped and committed suicide, would I have gone to Hell?'

Michael smiled again. 'No, John. No matter what sins you have committed in life, God always forgives them, provided that you are repentant of course.'

John scratched his stubbled chin as he pondered his next question. 'So, murderers, rapists and child abusers... they all go to Heaven?'

Michael puffed out his cheeks, his breathing becoming laboured as he did so. 'Like I said, if they are repentant and truly sorry for what they have done, then the Lord shall forgive them.'

John's shoulders dropped their stiff posture as he took in all of the information. 'Okay, so if they don't repent and are not sorry for their crimes, then what?'

'Then they are not worthy of God's love!' said Michael, again looking up at the night sky. 'This is how Hell gains its souls, though these are only in the most extreme of man's sins—the most heinous crimes of humanity.'

John thought for a brief moment. 'And what of those who have committed little sins like, I don't know, telling lies for example?'

Michael picked at the dry flakes of paint from the steel ledge. 'Trivial sins such as lies will not condemn you to the fiery lakes, I can assure you of that.'

There was another brief silence before the noise of angry car horns woke their separate trains of thought.

John turned quickly to Michael. 'Ah, but what about an eye for an eye? It does say that in the Bible after all.' He smiled, pleased with himself as he wagged his finger.

'Again, this is where the contradictions come into play,' said Michael as he ran his hands through his wet hair. 'As I said previously, the Bible has been dramatically altered over the centuries. An 'eye for an eye' was some mad monk's written justification to himself; he thought that as he was Holy it was okay for him to gain revenge for some wrong done to him. It was never actually written in the original scriptures.'

Michael contemplated the ever changing skies. Fierce snowflakes melted on his unlined, immortal face. He looked down at the water, at the thousands of individual tiny ripples that sprung outwards as each drop of rain touched its surface.

John was relentless in his pursuit. 'What about a soldier in war? He kills an enemy, which is still another human being.'

Michael pulled his eyes from the Heavens and gazed out far across the river. 'A soldier in war regardless of whether he kills or not is in fact safe, depending on his cause. You see, if he fights for a just cause, for example, a safer place for his people, or to rid the world of an opposition that wishes only to dictate and harm the innocent, then they have our vote.'

John pondered the answers for a while as he rubbed his white hands together in a feeble effort to warm himself up. 'Yes, but surely both sides in a war believe that their cause is just. So how do you separate the two—whose cause is right and whose is wrong?'

Michael looked at John angrily. 'Please, you are giving me a headache now,' he said, pleading with his hands for John to stop.

John's tongue toyed with his dry lips. Again he was confused by the Bible's contradictions. 'You said that whatever one does in life can be forgiven, if repented.'

'I know, I know,' replied Michael tiresomely as he continued to search the Heavens for stars amidst the dark clouds and peppering rain.

They sat again in complete silence for several minutes, staring at the metal chaos below them.

'So, how do you feel about things now?' asked Michael, more up-beat as he shifted his body on the ledge. 'Have I made things clearer for you?'

John continued to look downwards. 'I know that I can never be who I once was, those days have long gone. You did say that I had the choice, right? And if I do what I originally planned to do, then I can repent and go to Heaven. It seems like a win-win situation really, doesn't it?'

'Well, if you put it like that, then yes,' conceded Michael, a frustrated frown adorning his chiselled features. He looked sadly at John. 'You have completely missed the point of what all of this is. I have failed you.' The archangel gripped the collars of his woollen jacket and proceeded to shake the wetness from them. 'There is a bigger picture you know,' he said as he opened his arms wide, gesturing to include the world around him. 'Besides, what about your children, have you considered how they might react to your loss?'

John sniggered, his breath hovering in the air before fading. 'They don't give a shit!' he said loudly. 'They're old enough to get over it. In fact, they'll probably hate me even more as all they will be left with is the bill for my funeral!'

Even Michael couldn't help but smile as he found the statement mildly amusing.

'If that's what you really want to do, then I shall not stop you,' said Michael, resigned to the fact.

John looked back to Michael as he lifted his body up from the ledge. He steadied himself once again with his right arm, whilst using his left to balance. 'Michael, it has been an honour to meet an archangel and warrior such as yourself. I'm sorry for wasting your time; I am truly sorry for all that you are about to witness.'

Michael leapt up from the ledge and onto his feet. His jacket rode the wind as he stood next to John in a solid, almost superhero-like posture. 'Are you sure you really want to do this?' he asked one last time.

'Lord God Almighty, forgive me as I repent all of my sins!' John gazed up to the black sky. The snow pelted down stronger, like bullets battering the pair of them mercilessly. He turned to Michael's pained expression. 'Goodbye,' he mouthed quietly.

He closed his eyes, and let his body fall effortlessly from the ledge. The high pitched squeak of wet rubbery soles pierced the air as he disappeared. His life quickly flashed inside his fragile mind as he fell head first. His parents, his wife, the birth of his children; everything that was once good made a single tear run from his eyes. It ran cruelly over the side of his forehead as he managed a glance backwards. He could see the hurt visibly etched on Michael's face, the archangel's dark figure becoming ever smaller.

He hit the icy surface fast and hard. The impact winded him as he sunk further into the grey water. One thought entered his dying mind as the freezing liquid made its way agonisingly into his lungs. Peace and tranquility awaits.

His strong heart began fading, the beats slowing to a poor rhythm. Instinct gripped him; he began thrashing about wildly as he fought death. His blue lips parted lightly as a smile broke across his stiffening face. His eyes glazed over, rolling back into his head. His body went limp and floated to the surface, face down; it began bobbing along the vicious waters. John was dead.

John opened his eyes, still thrashing his limbs. A bright white light appeared in the distance. He paused for a second as he evaluated the situation, remembering what had happened. He rose to his feet and approached the pulling light. 'This is it!' he said aloud, excited.

There in front of him stood Michael. He stared at the archangel's dry clothes before pulling at his own, that were somehow equally dry. He smiled euphorically as he looked up at the tall celestial being.

'Well, you made it. I didn't think you would do it to be honest,' said Michael as he smiled back.

'Wow, I can see what you mean now, Michael,' said John as he looked all around, elated at the calm surroundings. 'I can feel the warmth extending from the glow. Is that Heaven beyond the light?'

Michael walked towards the human. The brooding presence accentuated by the looming feathery wings—enclosed the archangel within an ominous darkness. 'Not quite, my friend. Not quite,' he replied with a wicked grin.

Filled with awe, John looked up at Michael. With that, the whole environment began to transform. The warm white light vanished in front of his eyes. It was replaced by a harsh coldness as everything began morphing into large sheets of grey metallic steel. He spat empty words, coughing up only salty water. Violent screams echoed from every wall round him. Confusion was evident as he placed his crinkled hands over his bleeding ears.

'I don't understand, Michael. What is this?'

His face began to distort as he could feel an immense fear crawl over his skin. His hair now dripped with water that ran away from his shivering soul. Tall shadowy figures glided through a strange reddish mist that swirled hypnotically in the cool air. Their silhouettes began shuffling towards him.

He turned to Michael. 'Help me!'

Michael released a raucous laugh and shook his head. They always beg for help!

Suddenly, Michael's whole body began to change. The long curly black hair disappeared into baldness, substituted by a large grey bulbous head that now stood upon a stalk-like neck. The dazzling white smile was gone, a pencil-thin mouth replacing it. Feathers floated silently to the oily metal grating as the angelic wings fell apart.

John fell to his knees, fear and pain grasping him in a crushing embrace. Desperately, he grabbed hold of Michael's boots, but the black leather turned into slimy four-toed feet. Shocked, his mouth dropped open as he withdrew his trembling hands from the bizarre appendages.

He looked up at Michael, pleading. 'What's happening?' A psychological pain roared incessantly in his head. 'Michael?'

There was no Michael anymore.

The alien looked down with large black eyes at the pitiful sight before it. Pathetic human! Your species and their emotions are so easy to manipulate. You and your so-called "faith". Though one fact does remain true in your Bible, and that is any human committing suicide shall immediately be transported to Hell. Look around—I think you will love your new home!

John froze as the words entered his mind telepathically. He couldn't comprehend what was happening. The whites of his eyes lit up the darkness as the fear took control.

'Is this, is this Hell?' he stuttered, the pain in his head becoming unbearable.

The alien's thin body crept closer. It bent its head to one side. You catch on fast human—you will be a perfect addition to our studies.

John gazed upwards from his crumpled foetal position. 'If this is Hell, then who are you?'

The deep eyes thrust themselves down heavily upon the whimpering soul. You can call me whatever you wish, it doesn't matter anymore.

John's blood-curdling screams echoed those of the damned as the aliens clawed at his pale, trembling torso. All that remained was a trail of salty water as the vine-like fingers dragged him through the mist, and down the dim, tubular corridor.

Chapter 9

A Last Conversation

'I don't think I can take much more of this,' said Mark as he gathered the weapon tightly to his chest. 'When they come, can't they take us together?' He shivered at the thought. 'It's going to be horrendous for whoever's left.'

'It's going to be horrendous anyway, no matter what the outcome,' replied James, 'but I know what you mean.'

The men sat quietly for several moments, fidgeting with a nervous exhaustion as they each pondered their immediate futures.

'I know you are young, but are you married?' asked Mark, trying to deviate from his thoughts. 'Got any kids?'

'No, I haven't got around to the family bit yet.' James clawed at his facial stubble. 'Though looking back I agree with what the General said, you know, about being glad that he didn't have children… because of the current situation.'

Mark looked to the ceiling, watching as the mist toyed with the flush lighting frame. 'Yeah, hindsight is a funny thing. Besides, children are going to be a necessity if we are to survive as a race, that is. The population is going to need a serious boost if things are as bad in the outside world.'

'You're not wrong,' chuckled James. 'I think China will have to do away with their one child policy!'

Mark forced a laugh. 'At least Africa will be okay, they have them by the dozen out there!'

The light moment passed. 'What about you, married?'

'Divorced.'

'I'm sorry, I didn't mean to pry,' said James as he turned his muggy head and looked at the Professor.

Mark's eyes met with the younger man's. 'It's fine, we're still good friends. We have a young daughter, Erin, she's eight; I have her every other weekend, and we split the holidays.' His eyes began to glaze over as her image sat in his mind. He ran a hand through his thick peppered hair, down to the back of his neck. 'I hope that she's safe.'

'I'm sure she is, mate. Don't forget, we still don't know what's happening out there.' James gently patted Mark's knee with the tips of his fingers. 'She's probably tucked up in bed asleep, safe and sound.'

The thought brought forth an effortless smile that sprang from cheek to cheek. He hoped that James was right and that she was safe. Keep it inside, don't give these bastards a bigger incentive, or the satisfaction.

'What exactly do you do?' asked James. 'I know you're a Professor, at Stanford was it?'

'Yeah, have been for' He paused for a minute. 'I'm still getting fragments now and again, but I can't be 100% sure how long come to think of it.'

James shifted awkwardly on the floor as he sought a more comfortable position. 'The General talked about a time machine, was that for real?'

'Yeah, I guess so.'

'Okay, so what type of Professor would be needed to invent something like that?'

'A Theoretical Physicist I suppose.' Mark looked directly into James' eyes. 'Ah, yes. I must be a Theoretical Physicist!'

'There you go.' James bounced his head in respect. 'Must be a rewarding job I imagine.'

Mark changed the direction of the conversation. 'I would like to know what the General was getting at though. What did he mean when he said that "I would find out"?'

'I wouldn't know, Mark. Maybe it's better that you don't know either, eh?'

'It was an odd thing to say—he must have known something.' Mark bit his bottom lip cautiously as he paused for a moment. 'Have I done something wrong?'

James yawned as he shook his head. 'I wouldn't dwell on it too much. The only thing I find odd about it is the fact that the General was the only one who retained his memories, almost instantly it seems.'

'Yeah, I pondered that earlier, but put it down to his large build. Perhaps the mist, gas, or whatever it is, wasn't enough in terms of the ratio with his BMI.'

'BMI? I don't follow. What's that?'

'Body Mass Index. Imagine trying to tranquillise an elephant with a pea shooter, it won't work. It's the same principle with the dart. If it's not loaded with the correct dosage, then the elephant stays standing. Add the full dose to the dart and the elephant drops like a ton of bricks.'

'I love the analogy, Professor. You are definitely a University man, no doubt about it.'

'Yourself, what about you?' said Mark as the tiredness forced his head back against the wall.

'No kids, you know that. I'm not what you would call the "settling down" type.' He appeared distracted momentarily, as though deep in sad thought. 'I seem to meet someone, have a relationship with them for a few months and then it's over. Then I go out, meet someone new and start all over again. I can't see myself spending the rest of my life with the same person, there's too much going on in the world for that.' He sighed and took a deep breath. It was almost like he didn't believe his own words. 'It's just how I am, how I'm made.'

'No, my friend. I'll tell you why your life cycle spins like that,' Mark smiled, shaking his head in disagreement. 'It's nothing to do with how you're made, it's simpler than that. The reason you hop from relationship to relationship is because you are young.' He could sense James' deflated belief. 'It's all a part of youth, like a practice run until you do meet the right woman, the one. There is a specific person waiting out there, searching for you also. Trust me, you may think I'm mad, but you'll see, you'll know when your soulmate comes into your life.'

A false smirk masked James' true emotions. 'Well, I don't think that'll be happening soon, do you?'

Mark played with the weapon carefully as he rolled it around his fingers. He checked every millimetre of the steel, looking for an extra advantage, though he wasn't sure what he was expecting to find.

James brought his knees to his chest, and rested his dangling wrists upon them. 'Is it intact, did it get damaged in the fight?'

'Yeah, I think it's okay.' Mark stared hard at the gadget, his eyes pained from the effort. 'I hope so anyway, it came in extremely useful.'

James half shut his eyelids. 'Problem is they'll come for us with something bigger.'

'Sorry, but this is all we've got.'

James nibbled at the hard splinters of skin that congregated around his fingernails. 'I know, I'm not knocking it,' he mumbled.

'Next time I'll try all the bloody buttons on this thing! They might do something else, especially this one on the bottom here,' said Mark. Both men peered at the tiny hard silver button.

'Try it,' said James curiously. 'You won't know unless you try it.'

Mark's face winced at the thought. 'Christ, no! I have no idea what it is. It could release a deadly gas or something. No, it's not worth the risk. I'll wait for the Grey bastards, then try it.'

The watery sound shook James from another weak sleep. 'Who's there?'

'It's okay, it's me, I was only relieving myself,' came the voice that echoed back through the haze.

James felt a massive blast of fear leave his body. He leant back against the wall as the relief washed over him from head to toe, happy at hearing the Professor's voice.

Mark staggered back into view. 'Something has been bothering me,' he said as his hands felt for the wall. 'I was thinking earlier, back to when we were talking.'

'What about it?' said James, rubbing his forehead. 'What part specifically?'

Mark shuffled down next to James. 'Well, none of us knows why we were taken, right?'

'Yeah, and?'

'I'm a Professor of Physics, and the General, well, that speaks for itself. I think that Tom was someone more than we think. I mean, you saw his physique, he was no slouch; he ended up like that because of what happened to him. Then John, what did he do?'

James let out a quick, chuckling snort. 'I don't know, why?'

'Daniel was a bit, strange, shall we say. And what did you say that you did for a living?'

James thought for several seconds. 'I can't remember.' A quizzical look stretched across his angled face. 'Now that's bizarre. I can think back years, yet I don't recall what I did for a job. Anyway, staying on track, what's your point?'

'The point I'm trying to make is that we, those of us that recall our jobs, are in important positions in society. For example: the General in the military, I'm in physics, Tom's physique, I think that they are somehow linked.' Mark stared at James as he waited for a response. 'What do you think?'

'Are you saying that this isn't random, that we've been "selected"?'

'Yes. I think that we have been purposely brought here because of our backgrounds, our particular expertise maybe.'

James scowled at Mark's suggestion. 'So, what you're saying is that we've been selected. The General had military knowledge, you with physics and science.' He raised his hands, placing them behind his head. The stains underneath his armpits were now evident through his thin jacket, not that he knew, or would even care. 'Okay, I'll humour you. But we still don't know what the others did, or who they even were.'

'Yes, but it's possible, right?'

'Anything is possible, Mark. Though if you're suggesting that we have been taken to prevent, say, a future scenario? Well, that's a bit too much.'

'Yes. What if that is the point precisely?'

'Okay. But what scenario? Are you saying that we are to be executed because in the future our jobs, or important positions in society, will have some major effect on these slimy bastards? You know, throw a spanner in their works somehow?'

'What if?' said Mark with a shrug of his shoulders. 'It's only a theory, but a plausible one, no? 48 hours ago most of the world's population would have said that aliens and spaceships don't exist—now look.'

'True. But if you think these creatures have come back in time to kill us, heroes who topple an alien empire years from now? That's grasping at straws a bit, mate.' James looked to the floor. 'Sorry.'

Mark felt defeated. The one person that he thought might understand him, didn't. 'You're right, maybe I'm losing it completely. Perhaps I'm having a breakdown? Anyway, take no notice, it was just a strange feeling that I had, that's all.'

'What sort of feeling?' asked James curiously.

'I'm not sure, almost like I know something. It was a strong sensation that came back to me.' He paused as he collected his thoughts. 'What if I do know something, what if the General was right?

James turned to the Professor, whose face held a worrying expression. 'I guess we'll find out soon enough.'

The sounds of tiny insect pitter-patter broke the quiet as the two men sat, huddling themselves to keep warm. The strain was prominent, etched into their dazed and weary features. Their senses had become slowly accustomed to the terrible stench that wafted through the air; though they probably couldn't tell the difference between it and their own unwashed bodies.

'Where are you from, Mark?' said James with a scratch of his bedraggled dyed hair.

'Paignton originally, in Devon. Though the States has been my permanent base for the last, well, quite a while I think.' He cast his mind back home to his youth, and to the carefree attitude that saw him enjoy those gorgeous warm summer days before the new school term. The boat trips with his dad from Paignton harbour, those were fun times.

He thought of the 18th century harbour that rested along the western shores of Tor Bay, between Torquay and Brixham harbours. Surrounded by a lovely picturesque fishing village, which always brought the tourists flocking, its fairway approach lie on the port side, and not the standard starboard side. It was truly unique.

He remembered the day that he had chosen the cinema with his friends over one of the boat trips; the crippling sadness that had adorned his dad's face as he knew that their bonding adventures were at an end—that his son was growing up. How he didn't give it a second thought as he charged off with his friends. It was a great time when he was young, and he felt privileged for being allowed to experience it. But his dad's face...

'Reminiscing, eh? Wow, must have been nice.' James blew into his hands for warmth. 'Were you a surfer boy? I bet you were. That's why you moved to the States. Did you study over there, in America?'

The barrage of questions shook Mark from his memories. 'Yes and no,' he said, clearing his fuzzy past with a shake of the head. 'Most of my education was local before going to Oxford to gain my degrees and main qualifications. But America is where I always wanted to be. And yes, the surf is very appealing there, that I do remember.'

'That must have been strange?' said James.

'What?'

'Having a Cornish accent, and then arriving in the good ole US of A. Bet they had a field day with your accent to begin with!'

'You're not wrong,' chuckled Mark half-heartedly, almost painfully. 'But I always had a knack for adopting different accents whenever I stayed somewhere for a long enough period of time.'

'Makes sense. I was going to say that you don't have that much of an English twang. I thought that you might have been born there, in the States, before moving here.'

'No, no, no, I'm an Englishman, born and bred,' said Mark. 'You?'

James stared at the Professor, looking right through him as though he wasn't there. 'I still can't remember, my mind is blank. Every time I try to think, I get nothing except blackness.' He looked to the floor, frustration simmering as his mind raced. If only I could remember, it might add a bit of clarity and meaning to who I am. He raised his head; he could see Mark's dark eyes glaring at him through the smoky swirl. 'How is it that you can, and I can't?' he asked with a sad desperation. The need to know was becoming agonising to him.

'It's probably just how the brain works, James, that's all. We each process things differently. Your memories might come in one massive burst, whereas mine have been dribs and drabs over the course of our time here,' said Mark. 'We are all different.'

His attempts at an explanation still didn't have the desired effect. James appeared unsatisfied, this he could tell. But his words would have to suffice—he didn't have another theory to ease the increasing fragility within.

Outside the room, more screams reverberated down the corridor.

James' eyes shot up from the floor. 'What the fuck was that?' he said, alarmed as he looked to the door.

Mark heaved himself up from his slumped position, a worried look crossing his weary face. 'I don't think I want to know.'

The blood ran cold, chilling the bones. James looked to Mark, whose sagging skin hung from its frame. 'Was that another human voice?'

'Can't be sure with these bastards, it's past the point of know-ing whether they're playing dirty tricks or not.' The Professor's eyes searched the air. 'Could be another form of torture.'

He stood up and walked slowly towards the door, waving his hands as he sought focus through the mist. The cries seemed to have sub-sided. 'Can't hear anything, I think they've stopped,' he whispered, a twisted look upon his face as he strained to listen. He looked back across the room, searching for where James sat.

'Mark!'

The door panel lit up, stopping the Professor dead in his tracks. The thick door shot across, sucking out the haze. He watched as it began floating out and down the corridor. He started to back up one step at a time as the tall shadows grew through the cloudy veil. The wispy swirls parted slightly, just enough as four large eyes looked down upon him with hostile intent.

He frantically searched his back pockets for the weapon which, after a nervous few seconds, met his skin with its cold steel. He thrust it aimlessly forwards at the presence that he felt was approaching. The crackling light gave away his position. A thin arm shot through the mist, connecting with his head like a sledgehammer and sending him reeling to the floor. The device flew from his weakened grip.

Come here, human. It's your turn to die!

'Oh God, oh God,' said Mark, quivering as he frantically patted the floor, feeling for the weapon as the words reverberated around his skull. 'Arghhh,' he gurgled as a moist hand clasped his neck violently.

It tightened its hold with each human kick for survival, slamming him against the wall to tame the liveliness that fought for freedom. The alien brought its arm back; its eyes took in Mark's terrified expression as it held him face to face. For the first time, the Professor could feel hatred exuding from the creature as it absorbed his image. Its deep eyes, cold, hard, were a window to a soul filled with detestation, over-flowing with revulsion.

Mark struggled pointlessly. He tried to peel the aliens' fingers from his throat. The other shadowy figure loomed over the shoulder of the first, watching on as though enjoying the scene in a sadistic trance.

Heavy steps could be heard pounding the grating. James came hurtling out from within the mist, leaping at the side of the creature holding Mark. Even though its arms were thin and gangly, they were still strong as they failed to release the Professor. The second Grey swatted James to the floor like a fly. He lay there on his back, dazed and hurt, useless.

He lifted his head painfully, quickly realising that the darkness upon his face was due to the alien's long shadow. It stood over his head, keeping watch on him. James looked up at it, disheartened. In its hand was the weapon that Mark had dropped; its fingers entwined around the gadget. He turned his eyes towards Mark.

The fight in the Professor was fading. There was an ugly crunching sound as the alien slowly closed its hand. Mark's eyes remained wide, his face a deep shade of violet as the oxygen diminished. Sensing death, the alien released its iron hold from his damaged neck. It took a step backwards, watching on as the human held his throat, struggling for breath as he collapsed to his knees.

The alien gave Mark time to recover some composure, but the damage was done. He could hardly talk anymore except for a hoarse, wheezy crackle with each excruciating movement. He painfully climbed to his feet, sputtering hard as his vocal chords were now crushed. With his left hand clutching his throat, he reached out towards the alien with his right. Each time his arm was knocked sideways as the Grey mocked his every attempt. Without warning it threw its right arm directly at Mark's head.

The tears ran down James' creased face as he watched the shadowy forms helplessly. 'No, please, no.' Clang! He winced as the Professor's severed head flew to the floor; the body quickly followed, leaving behind a vertical bloody trail that spewed out from the neck as it slid down the wall. 'You fucking bastards, you fucking animals!' he cried, closing his eyes as he turned his head away.

The alien clutched the dead Professor's right ankle and proceeded to drag it towards the door. The other Grey walked away from James and lowered its lengthy frame, squatting as it picked up the decapitated head. It held it by the hair, away from its body, careful not to get any of the human's blood and brains upon its skin. It stopped and glanced at the weapon in its left hand, and then back at James. It flicked its arm out, sending the device in a crashing skid along the grating before the wall stopped its spinning momentum.

The door whizzed open, allowing the two creatures to pass through without breaking stride. The poor light added a brief glow to James' tear-streaked face. He watched Mark's body twist and turn as it was brutally dragged down the corridor's vast surface. The light vanished just as quickly as the door closed, returning the room back to its near dark state.

Chapter 10

Backwards Glance—Mark's Story

Professor Mark Bennett pulled at the cobalt blue tie knot in an attempt to loosen it from his stiff neck. He puffed out his cheeks, relieved at finishing the long dissection of his work. His mouth was extremely dry; he picked up the tall glass of still water before him, and sipped gently. The Head of the Theoretical Physics Department then took a deep breath. His dark brown eyes travelled the heads of the world's media who, sitting before him, chattered amongst themselves like excitable children.

A chorus of satisfied sighs filled the large beige conference room at Stanford University as the air conditioning kicked in once more. It whirred efficiently as it circulated amongst the many guests, giving instant relief to all who congregated at this historic press gathering.

Mark got the nod to continue. He smoothed his tousled greying hair into place with the palm of his sweaty right hand. A sharp cough cleared his raspy throat. He leant in towards the cluster of small microphones that sat upon the wooden podium, centred at the head of the room. The press pack stared back at him with the same astounded looks that they'd had for the last hour and a half. The room fell completely silent as they waited for the Professor to speak.

'Hello, ahem, excuse me. Hello again. If you wish to have more information on the mathematical breakdowns, and the quantum physics research that accompanies it, then you will find everything you need to know in the Progress of Theoretical and Experimental Physics journals which will soon be available. If not, then I suggest that you buy a copy of Time magazine.'

A stream of gentle laughter swam around the room as the camera flashes flickered incessantly, dazzling the Professor's vision.

'So, the math has been explained, or the boring bit as some may call such,' said Mark in his adopted Californian tongue as he gripped the edges of the podium. 'Now let's get on to the good stuff, the practical lessons.'

The crowd chuckled again, though this time there was a keen shuffling of backsides on folding wooden chairs. This is what they had all been waiting for.

Mark gestured to his three white coated colleagues to delicately wheel in the metallic, six-foot cuboid machine. Gasps climbed the air at the audacity of the proposal on offer before them.

Their shocked faces reminded him of Edvard Munch's famous painting, The Scream.

Mark beamed as he turned his reasonably athletic body towards the many faces. 'I gather that this is why you have all been so patiently putting up with me?' He let the apprehension build in the room for several seconds before continuing. 'Well, here it is. I give you the Wormhole Extender and Rotating Expansion device, or W.H.E.R.E. for short, though we here at the University prefer to call it the "backwards glance".'

With that, he grabbed a handful of the white sheet cover and threw it back over the top of the machine, watching as it fell gracefully to the floor. Tah-dah! His female colleague quickly gathered the sheet in a bundle, giving the Professor a grin as she passed by him.

A field of hands grew high as loud mutterings demanded immediate answers. Mark tipped his head towards the thin cross-legged journalist who sat in the front row.

'Hi Professor, Dan Finkelman from the Los Angeles Times. This is quite a boast, is it not?' he asked in a curious tone. 'I know that you all here at this prestigious University must have something special, otherwise the world's eyes wouldn't be watching. But is this for real?'

Mark smiled courteously as the hands rose again in a cacophony of eager pleads, like a class full of students begging to impress their teacher.

'Mr. Finkelman, it's a straightforward question so I'll give you a straightforward answer.' His eyes moved to include the whole room. 'I understand that you are restless from all of the previous jargon, I know that I am. But now I give you the gift of time travel to the past!' A lively grin pushed his dark eyebrows upwards as he returned his attention back towards Finkelman. 'Do you really think that I have spent the last 90 minutes acting out a prank?' he laughed. 'Yes, it's real.'

Another cluster of hands shot up. Mark circled the group with his right index finger. 'Erm… yes, you there.' He pointed towards the attractive blonde woman who sat a few chairs to the right of the balding Finkelman.

'Audrey Kleinmann from the New York Times. Forgive my under-enthusiastic colleague, Professor,' said Kleinmann with a disconcerted look to Finkelman, 'but to cut to the chase, when do we get a demonstration?'

Mark rubbed his hands together excitely. 'Thank you for your directness, Miss Kleinmann is it? I know this is what you all really wish to see, so here we go.'

Kleinmann nodded respectfully as she tapped her black digital recorder repeatedly against her tanned chin.

The room went silent once again as Mark approached the machine. He began to push several buttons that sent the device into a loud hum. His fellow colleagues tapped away on their computer keyboards as they entered in the required information; their hands bounced up and down at speed as they punched the plastic keys with force.

'As was said during the talk on the dynamics of the mechanism earlier, it manages to produce the equivalent energy of diminishing stars that, in space, have collapsed and folded. These would then fall into a rotating ring of neutrons that produces the centrifugal force needed for such an effort.'

A sudden intrusion derailed Mark's train of thought.

'I'm sorry to interrupt, Professor,' asked the fresh faced journalist who sat fidgeting with his pen and notepad. 'But centrifugal force, could you explain please?' He quickly realised his amateurish error.

Frustrated glances centred on the now embarrassed man as he sunk slowly into his seat.

'Yes, of course,' agreed Mark majestically. His glare hovered jokingly over the young journalist before continuing. 'For those who were not paying attention, think of a ball on a piece of string for example. Once you swing the ball, the string pulls on the ball causing it to follow a curved motion, this is called centripetal force.' He moved his arms in a series of explanatory gestures. 'Now the ball, which in our case is our mass, will tend to snap the string due to its mass and speed. The ball will then fly away from you, this is called centrifugal force. So, think of the ball being myself who, is swung around a black hole, a Kerr black hole in this instance, without a singularity, all the while following the rotation of the hole. The string, or centripetal force, will pull me towards the centre of the hole.' He stopped to take a breath, and gazed out at the sea of anticipation. 'Is everyone following me so far?' he asked, to which silence remained. 'Good. In a normal black hole this would be bad because of the singularity. Now, the singularity is the point in a black hole that would use centripetal force to pull me in and crush me. So, centrifugal force would be needed to send me away from the singularity once my mass snaps the string. But don't forget, the bigger the mass, the greater the force.'

A crowd of digital voice recorders stood firm in the air, surrounded by the clicking cameras. Mark turned and walked towards the large whiteboard that was fixed to the wall behind the podium. He picked up a red marker pen from its black plastic ledge, and proceeded to explain the science through a series of diagrams.

'Okay, this is why a Kerr black hole will be used. A Kerr black hole is a rotating hole that doesn't have a singularity. Instead, it has collapsed stars that become a ring of neutron stars spinning around the hole. Because of this ring there is no singularity, no point in the hole that would crush me, therefore I will be able to pass straight through the hole unharmed.'

Several appeased mumbles echoed around the room as Mark stared over the hall. He twitched as the dampness from underneath his armpits had dried into an uncomfortable stickiness on his light blue shirt. He clicked the red cap back on top of the marker pen and walked back towards the podium. Even on this warm August day, the sunshine began to seep through the white plastic venetian blinds, momentarily blinding several faces in the front row. He took a large gulp of water, and tried to remain openly confident.

'James Buckley from the Washington Post. Professor, what happens once you step through this "Kerr black hole"? Where do you go, end up?'

Mark raised his left index finger while quickly swallowing the water. 'This is the brilliant part, Mr. Buckley. Once the coordinates, from any part of the world around us today are entered into the computer, I shall be presented with a selection of events from past times that match up with these specific numbers. I can then pick a point in time that I wish to visit. Think of it like standing on a bridge over a motorway, watching the heavy traffic pass through all day long. In this case the "traffic" is in fact every period in time; from Nazi Germany to Alexander the Great, Joan of Arc to the Jurassic era. You name it, I can go there.'

'My God, this is incredible, if it is possible of course,' added Buckley as his blue pinstriped suit crumpled some more. 'How far back have you been in your tests, and what have you seen?'

'Well, we have seen it all as you can imagine. We've been like a child with a new toy!' said Mark excitably. 'Though we haven't seen things in the way that you might think. So far for our safety we have only sent through cameras to record events. This way we have been able to determine the differing levels of danger.'

Buckley fired the Professor a derisory look before continuing in a concerned voice. 'I'm sorry, Professor, you mean that this technology is untested on humans?! How do you know it is safe? How do you know that what you touch won't have an adverse effect on history; will it alter anything in our here and now for example?'

Grumbles rose from the gathering as Mark attempted to quieten his audience with outstretched hands. 'It is extremely safe, Mr. Buckley. We here at Stanford have done our sums. History will be made today, I can assure you of that,' he replied confidently. 'To answer your second question? No, nothing can be affected. We have been studying this as best as we can for the last four years. We have recorded thousands of non-specific single events from many different eras and times. These were all with the intention of seeing if our cameras, or interventions, caused any effect, either short term or long term on the futures that followed said events. Now, whether these were small, large, one minute, one hour, day, week, or whatever, these have all been thoroughly tested to exhaustive limits.'

Buckley whispered under his breath in a sceptical manner. His round face creased and wrinkled, like that of a bulldog puppy as he adjusted his thick rimmed mahogany glasses. 'Okay. But when you've reached your desired location in time, well, how do you get back?'

Mark waggled both of his index fingers in mock gun style, aimed at Buckley. 'I'm glad that you asked that.' He dug his right hand into the back pocket of his deep blue jeans, and pulled out a small square black gadget that looked like a television remote control. 'This Black Hole Location Remote, or B.H.L.R., we like our acronyms here, will send a signal back to the device. Once I press this green button, the computer and the machine will instantly know where the signal has been emitted from. This in turn will let it, and the team, know where I am, and if I need an exact sized hole from whence I originally came.'

'So, it acts similar to say… radio waves for example?'

Mark paused for a split second. 'Yes, a bit more complicated, but in a roundabout way I suppose.'

Buckley's full lips bent downwards as he gestured with his large head, seemingly satisfied by the Professor's answers.

The room erupted into chaotic voices as the media tried to comprehend exactly what they were about to witness. All eyes became glued on Mark as he assembled his team around the machine. He turned and faced the crowd, to which hushed silence immediately followed.

'You there, Madam,' he asked directly, prompting the red headed middle-aged woman who sat amongst the journalistic elite. 'Pick a path from the past.'

The woman looked round, slightly self-conscious at being singled out before straightening her posture. 'Rosemary Phillips from the BBC World Service. You wish for me to pick a "path", from any past walk of life?'

'Yes, Rosemary.'

All eyes in the room burned her soul with envious glares.

'Okay, let me think.' Phillips thought for several seconds, fiddling with her media identification pass before smiling. 'I've got it!' she exclaimed in a clear English twang which drew excitement. 'The Crucifixion of Jesus Christ!'

The room collectively inhaled.

'Excellent choice, Rosemary. I couldn't have picked a better path myself. This is one of the rare ones that we chose not to view, out of respect for the many religious implications that it could conceive,' said Mark, addressing the rest of the audience. 'I assume that there are no objections from any devout persons here?' The faces all consumed one another, desperately hoping that all hands remained down. 'Excellent. Ladies and gentlemen, please stay seated for the next several minutes as the team prepare for the path.'

The team of Mike Daniels, Joseph Keller and Mia Long helped Mark get into the simple military style combat suit. The dark olive green outfit consisted of various pockets equipped with cameras and survival tools. A camouflage rucksack had been pre-packed; it was filled

Chris Botragyi

with the necessary food, a digital camera, and above all else security and first aid supplies needed for the potentially hazardous, unknown journey.

'Are you ready for this, Mark?' asked Keller in a firm voice.

Mark could feel his heart pushing out of his heaving ribcage. He felt nauseous as his limbs began to tremble. He looked at Keller's youthful face which, despite glistening with thick beads of sweat, remained relatively calm.

'Relax, Mark. You need to slow your heart rhythm down,' interrupted Long. 'I know it's going to be scary, but you've got to calm down. If you don't, you'll be going into shock before we even get started!'

Mark nodded, trying to take deep breaths as he closed his eyes lightly.

Daniels' rough grip continued to pull and prod the Professor. He made sure that every camera and piece of equipment was in its place, and working.

Long's oval face came into Mark's eye-line. He stared at the pretty, short haired brunette for a while. I'm going to die today.

She used her slender hands to gently cup his quivering face. 'It'll be alright, Mark. Remember, you've been trained for this. Stick to the plan and you will be fine, and tonight we'll all be celebrating your Nobel Prize for Physics award.'

Mark opened his eyes, taking comfort in the soft red lipstick smile that warmed his heart. He suddenly felt a tranquility pass through him as she playfully slapped his cheek.

She smiled again. 'You're almost good to go.'

'Okay, let's do this.' He puffed out his cheeks and ran his fingers through his wavy hair.

Daniels helped place the military style helmet on his head. He could feel the tech expert's warm breath fan his sweaty face as he checked the camera that protruded from the green headwear. He looked admiringly at the bald, overweight former soldier. Daniels knew his stuff alright, they all did.

157

sdf333s

'Doesn't this gear come in any other colours?' asked Mark, half-jokingly. 'After all, I'm going to Jerusalem, not the jungle.'

'Good point,' replied Keller as he spun around, his foppish brown hair semi-covering his pale blue eyes. 'Here.' He threw the white sheet that had previously covered the machine. 'See what you can do with this.'

Mark shrugged his shoulders as he caught the sheet. He began folding it into the rucksack anyway.

The machine still hummed and whirred as the assistants stepped back, allowing Mark to face the throng. He raised his voice to compensate.

'What we shall attempt to do now is to open a small Kerr black hole. This will be achieved by the machine, that itself will act as a mini Hadron Collider. Using Einstein's theory of relativity, the particles will travel close to the speed of light before smashing into each other. As these particles fly around the collider they begin to warp space and time. They will then start to focus each others' energies which shall "open" the portal. Now, the faster these particles travel, the greater the mass. This means that we can control the size of the portal that will open.'

Again, whispers sailed around the room. Mark couldn't work out if the media were impressed, or if they thought he was insane.

He turned and nodded to Keller, who began furiously thrashing at the computer keyboard. His long manicured fingers danced effortlessly as they retrieved the information for the coordinates, dates and year required for the destination.

'31° 47'00' N 35° 15'03' E; these are the coordinates for the Mount of Olives, in Jerusalem,' shouted Mark over the throbbing metal as he craned his neck from the bright computer screen. 'This is near where Jesus was reported to have been crucified, though at that time it was outside of the city.' He looked back at the screen, then back to the audience. 'I shall be transported to the Mount of Olives, to which I will travel through the Kidron Valley and on to the East Temple Mount. Once there I head to Golgotha, the place of the Crucifixion, which

today is more commonly known as the Church of the Holy Sepulchre.'
He waited for the next set of information to follow. 'Okay, I shall be
going back to Friday 3rd of April, erm… AD 33.'

Suddenly, there was a flash. The room shook and frightened cries
came from within the crowd of seated bodies.

Long held up her hands and appealed for calm. 'It's okay, but please
stay seated for your own safety, and ours.'

The audience remained half stood, half sat. There was a loud crackle,
like the amplified sound of a fly frying on an electric insect repeller,
as a 12 inch tear materialised in the air. A cold blast exited the rip as it
gradually began morphing into a cylindrical spinning shape; it grew
larger with each rotation, slowing as it reached its maximum five foot
diameter.

Mark looked to each of his colleagues' faces in turn. He instantly felt
that each one portrayed false, confidence-lacking smiles as the gust
from the hole blew their hair and clothes in all manner of directions.

Long mouthed the words "good luck" to him as she shielded her delicate eyes with a pair of clear plastic glasses. He looked to the retreating
crowd and gave a nervous thumbs up. Closing his eyes he ducked and
stepped through the coiling portal, and into the infinite blackness…

Mark heard another loud pop as the space began to rotate before his
squinting eyes. White specks elongated into semi-circular lines that
stretched endlessly. He felt violently sick as his head started to spin.
There he stood, in the enormous centre of this black hole as events
from all the different centuries of life swamped his brain in a drowning
pool of imagery. They flashed up in large windows, like billions of
television channels all waiting to be selected for the desired viewing.
The pre-programmed times, dates and coordinates went to work. In a
split second, numerous images were presented directly in front of his
blurry, fading vision.

'Yes, the Crucifixion, of Christ,' he stuttered as he fought to stay on
his feet.

Complete silence followed.

Bright sunshine struck his face as he staggered out of the spinning swirl of blackness; sweat immediately gathered upon his lined forehead. He peeled off the plastic protective glasses, the black elastic twanging as he tugged them from his head. Slowly, he stepped onto the water deprived lands that were the Mount of Olives.

He raised his left hand loosely in front of his eyes in an attempt to block the blazing sunlight. He peered between his fingers before averting his gaze. The hole was gone. A feeling of sickness rippled through his stomach, forcing him to his hands and knees. He retched, vomiting up the liquids that he had previously drank. He watched as the grateful earth sucked up the watery contents and bile. Regaining his breath, he looked at his watch; 8:25 a.m. glowed back at him in green neon as he shielded the glass from the light. He was still disoriented as he tried to recover his equilibrium. He slipped the protective glasses into the rucksack, and pulled out the green water bottle. He quickly took a long drink which eased his sudden dehydration.

The helmet cam had to go, it was way too hot. Add the fact he would stick out like a sore thumb if he was spotted. He pulled the white sheet from the rucksack and splayed it outwards before wrapping it around his heavily clothed body. The heat was excruciating as the layers began to take their toll. He knew that he shouldn't remove any of his clothing as the risk of leaving something behind was too great. Even though the tests had proved that nothing would be affected by something as simple as a lost t-shirt, he didn't want to take the chance, he himself still had reservations. Besides, he didn't have the room in his rucksack anyway.

Just get on and deal with it. He started the journey through the Kidron Valley.

He stopped for another drink amidst the heat. A quick glimpse at his watch told him that it was 9:10 a.m. He had been trekking the gruelling, gravel strewn valley for around 40 minutes. He looked around cautiously before sighing in amazement as the valley appeared to carry for miles into the distance. It was another good opportunity for him to take some pictures of the surroundings on his digital camera. To the sides of the valley thick old trees stood firm, even in the sparse conditions. Gazing back, he snapped away at the crude handmade crosses, fascinated as they seemed to bob up and down in the sea of graves that drifted across the dirt hills. A touch of sadness washed through his sweat soaked body, causing the hairs on his skin to rise. He knew that he was close as he looked forwards, at the East Temple Mount.

His relaxed demeanour was soon interrupted by loud noises. He turned sharply as the raucous sounds stung his sensitive ears. The globules of salty water ran from his skull, curving down his face as he listened intently. He took backwards steps behind the trees off the path. He remained out of view, starting to become agitated. He gently slid the camera and water bottle back into the sides of the rucksack, then tried to blend with the scenery.

The thunderous vibrations became louder as many feet trampled the parched earth. From his position he could see Roman soldiers bypass the temple on their march towards Golgotha. The gold in their tunics reflected fiercely in the blazing sunlight. Perspiration ran profusely from underneath the brass helmets that adorned their wet heads. A baying crowd followed swiftly behind. He bent his neck, desperate for a sign of Jesus which, he knew, would come soon enough.

Mark's heart thumped as the top of the newly made wooden cross jabbed the warm air. It jutted up and down as it entered his vision repeatedly before disappearing. The strands from the scourge whips darted in and out of sight with each vicious, slashing strike. Flesh dangled grotesquely from the razor sharp metal and bone fragmented tips that were attached to its leather tassels. With each attack the glimmering shards got duller as fresh blood coated the unrefined weapons. The shadowy form carrying the cross cried as it struggled to remain on its feet.

He flitted between the trees, keeping a healthy distance from the crowd as he tried to direct his small shoulder cam towards the masses. I hope that you are recording this, Caravaggio's paintings of the flogging are correct!

The hike up to Golgotha was unbearable. He dug his boots in firmly as he ascended the mount. The intense heat seemed determined to break him; the effort was immense as he staggered with the heavy rucksack. Suddenly, 300 yards ahead, the people stopped. He looked around quickly, pulling out a creased map as he searched for a suitable location to watch the events unfold. According to his position on the paper he noticed that the Garden Tombs were nearby. This was where Jesus was to be buried, for the second time. This would give him some necessary cover for now.

He climbed awkwardly to the top of the tombs, digging his hands into the dry surface as he retained a firm grip. He collapsed onto his knees, exhausted as he reached the top. Grimacing, he wriggled out of the cushioned nylon shoulder straps that had twisted into his sore flesh. He waited for a moment as he tried to regain his breath.

The rucksack lay in the dust next to him as he sat crouched, looking down upon the crowd. Lumps of dry mud rolled speedily away from him at the intrusion. Small trees and wasting greenery offered some minor protection from the eyes of Jerusalem. He pulled the helmet cam from the rucksack and positioned it carefully on his head. Then, he synchronised the recording settings with the shoulder cam, followed by the digital camera. He began taking pictures of the ancient scenes, clicking away like a maniacal tourist. He removed his eyes from the view finder and paused for several seconds.

From this point forwards, history books will no longer contain drawings. They'll contain the exact pictures of the events themselves!

A stench of sweat, rotting fruit and human faeces hung in the air. Mark was continuously swatting the flies from his sticky face with one hand while attempting to gather information with the other. His body squirmed from the overbearing heat that engulfed his skin.

A horrific high pitched scream penetrated the stifling atmosphere. Mark cringed as the sound sent a shiver down his spine. He raised his head for a better view, seeking to rise above the verbal spewing that was aimed at the centre of the controversy. Again, the Roman soldiers held back the people as they demanded blood; their spear tipped pilums thrusted back and forth in their attempts to steady the clamouring waves of aggression.

The howls of a wounded animal sprang from within the exuberant crowd, echoing around the enclosed area of the tombs. The Professor's eyes welled up as all the literature, paintings and text that depicted these scenes flashed through his mind. Even though he couldn't see what was happening, he knew the horrors that Jesus was suffering. He dropped his head in shame as tears began to congregate in the corners of his eyes. His body heaved and jerked, reverberating at the sound of each anguished wail.

He composed himself before glancing over his crossed arms that lay in the soil. Each movement caused a tiny dust cloud to form around his clammy face, forcing him to wipe his grit-covered features. He used his camera to zoom in on the mob as the heavy wooden cross was placed flat upon the ground. He stared on as the Roman centurion ordered the removal of several long spikes from a shabby brown leather satchel, along with what looked like a worn claw hammer.

'This is it, here we go,' he whispered as the soldiers circled the cross.

He could hardly hear what was being said as the shouting continued.

A grey bearded man in beige robes begged and pleaded with the soldiers. 'I am Joseph of Arimathea,' he declared before dropping to his knees.

Mark's mouth fell open. 'Bloody hell, I can't believe it, that's Joseph of Arimathea!' he said excitedly, yet aloud for the benefit of both video cameras.

His temptation couldn't hold. He crawled on all fours through the harsh dirt as he strived for an advantage. He cautiously rose on his knees for a better look, while simultaneously wrenching his neck muscles to their limits.

'Oh God, oh fucking hell!' He fell onto his backside, his feet kicking out in the filth as he fought to move away from what he had just seen. 'W-w-what's happening?' He felt violently sick as he shook uncontrollably. He placed his hands over his mouth to suppress the raw emotions as his brain tried to comprehend, to filter, what his eyes had relayed back to it. He clambered back to his original position, desperate to focus the cameras on the playing spectacle. 'My God, are you getting this?' he whimpered in a cracked tone to the shoulder cam's audio.

There, being dragged onto the cross by the Roman soldiers was Jesus Christ, the Son of God. Mark once again recoiled in horror at the sight. The supposed "Jesus", that everyone had come to worship for the last 2000 years, lay not far from view in the dusty, stone-filled land. This was not what he had expected, nor could ever have imagined. He still couldn't stop trembling as the enormity of what was happening before his eyes skewered his fragility.

Animalistic whines pierced the sky as the seven-foot tall, grey humanoid was lashed again and again by the soldiers. Brown treacle-like blood oozed from the countless lacerations that criss-crossed its slender, leathery-skinned body. The disturbed crowd threw rocks and stones at the cowering creature; their verbal abuse cruel, spat like arrows of hatred. A length of sharp thorns had been wrapped tight around its skinny neck; this was no crown, it had been used as a collar for a leash. Every movement it made caused a distressing wince as the needles dug in deep.

The soldiers grabbed the creature's long spindly limbs, spreading them outwards with force as they held it down. Its huge black eyes seemed agonised, innocent as its pencil thin mouth bleated painfully like a sacrificial lamb. One of the soldiers took the iron hammer determinedly, hovering it over the rusted spike that was placed upon its bony wrist. Its four-fingered hand juddered with each formidable blow.

THUD, THUD, THUD, THUD!

Mark felt queasy again as he watched the hammer bury the spike home. The alien screamed as its syrupy blood spattered the nearest soldiers' faces. They cursed it with obscenities as they kicked and stamped angrily on its bleeding torso, which encouraged the crowd even more. They continued to place the remaining spikes through the other wrist, then one through both feet as members of the crowd continued to spit and taunt the wailing extraterrestrial.

He narrowed his eyes as he zoomed in on the camera. He watched as Joseph's sorrow stricken face pleaded with the soldiers to relent their violence, only to be pushed back aggressively. A young woman adorned in a red robe stood side by side with Joseph; she too appealed for the madness to cease. Her sprouting red hair bore the hallmarks of her fiery nature as she attempted to grab at the soldiers, to gain their attention in relinquishing their cruel actions. Mark looked on in contorted awe as this passionate woman fought to protect the alien.

'I pray that all of this is being bloody recorded, because that's Mary Magdalene!' he said to the camera again before pulling his face away, still shaking in fear and amazement.

The creature tried to move its head as it struggled to understand why this was happening. The same bleating sound left its weak mouth repetitively. Its withering body, now battered and broken, desperately fought to escape, but the pain caused it to cry out at every attempt.

Mark dropped his aching head to the ground and began crying hard. 'Why, why do we do this? We don't deserve to thrive as a species.' The tears ran fast from his stinging eyes, leaping from his face to his hands. He looked to the Heavens for answers as the being roared out from its latest torture. He cupped his ears with his grubby hands, he could take no more. 'We deserve to watch the world burn, we deserve only death.'

His guilt at not being able to do anything far outweighed his need for personal advancement. He placed his hands in the earth, clenching handfuls as he smashed and ground his fists over and over. His mind was frazzled, and it ached with a sorrowful weight. Slowly, he pushed himself to regain some sanity and focus on why he was here in the first place.

The four metre long wooden cross was heaved upright on broad ropes by the soldiers. There it stood, sickeningly proud between two terrified men who were also being crucified. Their empathetic looks towards the creature only served to weaken their own chances of survival.

Individuals from within the mob were still throwing rocks and debris at the alien as it groaned loudly. One of the soldiers suddenly rammed his long pilum into its side, snapping off the handle several inches below the spear tip. The sound that left its mouth shattered Mark's soul, and would haunt him until his dying days.

Mark lay in a dazed heap after passing out from heat exhaustion. The sun continued to glare down upon his static body, frying his bare hands in the hot soil.

The cries gradually subsided as Mary Magdalene and Joseph of Arimathea tried to sooth the creature's splintered mind. Its foreign organs pushed partly through the torso wound, glistening in the light with a slimy moisture. She wept as she serenely bathed its slender four-toed feet with cool water. Joseph looked up as the vultures began to circle the hazy skies. They cast a foreboding sense of death.

After a few hours, Mark opened his eyes gingerly. His sweat matted hair began to itch from the grime that centred within his scalp. He placed his bruised and burnt hands over his tired face, and wiped the sweat from his troubled brow. His moral boundaries could not grasp why people did what they did. It kept playing over in his muggy head like a broken record. How can humanity be so cruel and heartless?

He looked at his watch, it said 14:55 p.m. There was no letup in the oppressive heat as he began to gather his belongings. He took one last sad look at the bloodied body that clung to the wooden structure. He looked on dejectedly as Joseph and Mary still knelt, praying at the foot of the cross. Their distraught faces had shed a lifetime of tears. The alien wheezed and whimpered with each soft dabbing from the wet rag that she used. Her efforts to add some moisture to its dry wrinkled skin were not working.

Mark looked through the camera again. Even from the distance he could see that the creature's chest wounds had stopped bleeding. All that remained was an emaciated body full of deep gashes and flayed skin. The local insects got a good feed as they flocked together, happily buzzing amongst the few broken ribs that had torn through its side.

Devastated cries left Mary's sun exposed lips, the alien had breathed his last breath. Joseph held her back in an effort to console her. Its heavy head had flopped forwards, its eyes now a shade of light grey as the dark flicker of life had vacated them. What was left of the people celebrated amongst themselves.

Mark's lips quivered as the sorrow and shame crept over his entire body, filling his throat and heart with a strong burning sensation.

Almost instantly, a strange cooling in the air caused the Professor to shiver and look upwards. The brightness quickly began to disappear as an eerie darkness gradually ate the sky, blotting out the sun. The ground began to quake, followed by a dense humming sound. He looked down at his desert-booted feet as he tried to steady himself.

Hysteria broke out within the pack as the soldiers failed to keep order. Mark stared as arms were raised at 45° angles. Fear soared high from not only where he was, but from all around as the clear blue skies continued to turn a sinister black. The stalking gloom swam overhead, swallowing the land as he looked on. There, over the entire valley, came an approaching spacecraft. The gigantic metallic disc floated with little effort, though moved menacingly as it headed towards Golgotha.

'This can't be happening,' he said, snapping randomly away on his camera. 'T-this isn't in the Bible?!'

He felt faint as he quickly returned to packing the rucksack; he was careful not to forget anything amidst the mass panic before climbing sluggishly down from the tombs. He tilted his shoulder cam up at the enormous craft, which he estimated to be at least a mile in diameter. He couldn't hang around any longer, he knew that he had to get out, and fast.

He tightened the white sheet around his damp body, wincing at the uncomfortable chafing that his clothes made over the wetness. His heart beat dangerously as he scrambled down the dirty trail. Tired legs felt like lead as they struggled to form a regular rhythm, it was almost like he had forgotten how to run. His windpipe became clogged from the flying dust and earth, causing him to heave. He hardly looked back as he descended through the Kidron Valley, and back to the Mount of Olives.

'Keep going, keep going,' he kept repeating as he desperately tried to hold the weighty rucksack in place upon his painful right shoulder.

He didn't care who saw him anymore as the helmet fell from his head. He quickly managed a sliding U-turn in the gravel, grabbing at it with his left hand as it rolled clumsily away. All he thought about was getting home, and away from the grisly din that peppered the air from afar. The putrid smell of burning flesh and ash shot up his nose, jabbing his senses. God only knew what was happening to the people in Golgotha, because he sure as hell didn't want to know.

His body compass was all over the place. He wished that he was physically fitter as he fought to refrain from vomiting. With hands on hips, he spun in a full circle as he searched for the rough destination of his original arrival. In a panic he scoured the map, fingering the crease-riddled paper in desperate arcs as he scanned for the exact location.

'Shit, the remote,' he said, patting down his clothing, 'where is the remote?'

He looked back across the valley and at the shadowy disc. His hands frantically searched the pockets for the remote control. Finding it in his upper arm pocket, he juggled the plastic square in mid-air. His eyes followed its every move as it slipped in and out of his swollen fingers before he grabbed hold of it. He pointed it without aim, squeezing the round green button apprehensively, praying that it started the process for his journey home.

'Come on!' He continuously pressed the button impatiently. He cast a glance back at the alien ship again, all the while shaking the device angrily. 'Come on!' A small green light pulsed brightly from the remote. Momentarily relieved, he knew that back home they had received the signal.

Stones and dry mud rose from the vibrating ground as a tear began forming behind him. The magnetic field from the approaching hole interacted with the remote control's built-in magnetism. It forced Mark's arm, and then his body to spin round to its position. It yanked him forwards, like a powerful dog on a leash leading its owner on a merry dash.

Blackness blended with the remaining sunlight that caused a gold and coffee coloured effect as the swirling began. He felt dizzy as it dragged him towards the small spinning hole that had opened with a series of static, crackling blasts. He removed the rucksack from his pain-fraught shoulder and slung it wildly into the blur. He collapsed, falling head first into the hypnotic kaleidoscope.

A loud snap forced the journalists and photographers to crouch for cover. The tear opened within the room, like a transparent knife had slashed the air in an identical position to where its predecessor had been. Gasps sounded all around as the split grew outwards, turning into a hole that spun the scientists' sheets of paper and light objects within the air.

Keller watched as Mark fell through the hole. 'My God, we've done it!' he celebrated as the Professor dropped to the floor with a hefty thump.

Keller hammered the buttons of the machine which powered it down with a series of loud humming drones, each quieter than the last. The black hole ceased spinning and began reversing its motion, rewinding itself to a single point before vanishing. It was as though someone had stitched up the air with an invisible needle and thread. The hundreds of sheets of white paper floated to the floor like crisp, giant snowflakes.

Long and Daniels dashed over to where Mark lay, quickly followed by Keller. Daniels forcefully pulled the rucksack from the Professor's hand and pushed it away. Long gently cradled his aching head in her lap, stroking his feverish brow as everyone in the room looked on.

The photographers' cameras snapped away. Shadows flickered on the walls as a relentless stream of photos were taken—it was enough to cause an epileptic fit in the healthiest of people.

Mark looked up into Long's eyes, shivering as though the temperature had dramatically fallen. Without warning he vomited down the front of the dust stained sheet that he wore. Long turned his head sideways to prevent him from choking.

'It's okay, Mark, you're home now.' She soothingly stroked his grimy hair. 'Where have you been all this time? We were worried sick.' Mark tried to speak, but couldn't. 'Can we get some medical help here please?' she requested with a firm shout.

'Well done buddy, you've made history today. You'll be on the front of every magazine and newspaper in the world tomorrow,' added Keller enthusiastically as he carefully removed the camera from Mark's left shoulder.

Mark reached out for the camera, swiping through the air with an open hand as Keller's exuberance beamed down at him.

'No, Keller!' said Mark weakly as his voice croaked. 'Destroy that camera, destroy them all.'

'Are you serious?' A puzzled smirk sat upon Keller's face. 'This footage will be the greatest thing ever recorded, ever seen!'

Mark grabbed at Daniels' arm as the tech whiz continued to remove the strappings and gadgets from his body. He stared glassy eyed at the thick set, middle-aged man. 'Daniels, get that camera off Keller. Don't let anyone see it before I can explain what's on the hard drive.'

Long glanced her head sideways as she subtly motioned to Daniels. He leapt to his feet with purpose and walked quickly towards Keller. He calmly placed a large arm around his colleague's lower back as not to cause any concern amongst the journalists.

'Don't show it, Keller,' whispered Daniels sternly into the assistant's left ear. 'Mark says not to show it yet.'

Keller looked down at Mark, who in turn gestured for him to come over to where he lay. Daniels walked Keller back military style, like he was escorting a prisoner to his cell. The two men knelt down beside Long. All three strained to listen, but the raucous squawk of jumbled media questions took precedence.

'What is it, Mark, why don't you want us viewing the video footage?' asked Keller quietly, intrigued.

Mark placed a hand on each of the two men's forearms. He was cautiously aware of the prying ears.

'It's alright, Mark, you can tell us,' said Long in her velvet-toned voice.

'You can't… you can't show the world that footage. It's not what you think,' said Mark with effort as his dry throat had ceased to work properly.

Keller's blue eyes arrowed in on the Professor's exhausted, filth covered face. 'Tell us, what did you see, was it amazing?' he rambled excitedly. 'Did you see all the classic Biblical figures?'

Mark's face contorted as his eyes widened with confusion. 'It's not what you think. Jesus… No Jesus Christ.'

The three of them looked at each other with baffled frowns. The Professor narrowed his eyes in discomfort as the endless stabs of camera flashes temporarily blinded him. Daniels grabbed at the glass of water from the podium, almost knocking it over. He delicately held the glass to Mark's cracked lips; he gulped the water down greedily. He took several deep breaths, spluttering as he drank the liquid too quickly.

'It wasn't Jesus that they nailed to the cross, the Bible doesn't tell the true story.' He coughed hard as the water ran heavily down his throat, choking him. 'The ancient races of the past, like the Sumerians…' Long lifted his head slightly as he coughed again. 'Like the Sumerians, they were right. Their drawings of beings and spaceships on their archaic stone tablets are correct! Jesus was a story written to cover the truth of what really happened, and for good reason.'

Again, the three all looked to one another.

Long shook her head with a confused smile. 'I don't understand, Mark.'

'Jesus wasn't crucified on the cross!' whispered Mark bitingly. 'Don't you get it? It wasn't a human being, it was a fucking grey alien that suffered that fate! If this gets out it will be the end of civilisation, period! The impact on religion and faith will be irreparable, it will fold in on itself; the world as we know it will end. Like I said, they covered it up for good reason. Even they, 2000 years ago, could foresee the potential dangers that we now face.' He raised his right arm painfully and pointed at the machine. 'Destroy that device, no good can come from it. It will only bring a new pain and suffering into the 21st century.' Mark's vision clouded before he passed out.

The three looked at each other for a third and final time. This time though, the look was one of ultimate dread.

Chapter 11

Checkmate

James sat on the floor with his hands either side of him in the dirt, sobbing like a child. His fragile state had now reached fever pitch, he was on the brink. As the last man remaining, this terrified him to epic proportions. He zipped up the thin cotton jacket that he wore; it barely added any extra warmth to his cold body. His tears had fallen down the front of the material, drawing in the wetness as it blotted.

He placed the back of his head against the wall; the coolness eased his exhausted mind for several seconds. Closing his tired eyes, the violent deaths of the other humans played over. The scenes raced around his skull, quickening the unravelling of his sanity. The end was inevitable—he knew this, there was no denying it any more. He continued to cry as the full realisation hit him. Every minute that passed could be his last, it could be the time when they came for him. He placed his head in his hands, and raked them backwards through his hair. Shaking, he suddenly felt nauseous. Sickness rose in his stomach, forcing him to all fours as he gagged several times. Nothing vacated his body, there wasn't anything left.

The effort left him even more drained. He brushed the palms of his hands with his fingers, desperate to remove the grease that stuck defiantly. When this failed to work, he scraped them down his trouser legs in an angry last stand. Satisfied, he licked the salty taste from his lips before using his jacket sleeve to wipe his eyes.

Every conversation, no matter how trivial, now seemed a distant memory. The scuttling across the metal floor appeared amplified in the silence as he sat alone, multiplying his paranoia as he listened intensely. He hauled himself to his feet to escape the insects—after all, he still didn't know if they were poisonous or not.

He began pacing the room's perimeter in an anti-clockwise direction, dragging his right hand across the wall as he went. This is the end! He stopped on his third rotation. His left boot had caught the edge of an object and sent it spinning across the grating. His heart drummed heavily before he realised that it was the weapon. He hurried furiously across the floor with his arms held out, swimming through the mist as he hunted the device.

'Come on, where are you?' he said, panicking as he dropped to his knees in an agitated search. Forgetting the insects, he patted the floor area in and around the direction of where he thought the sound had trailed. 'Please God, help me find it.' He was becoming increasingly distressed as the minutes ticked by, though his worn limbs had found an adrenaline-fuelled second wind as he groped frantically. 'Yes!' he exclaimed loudly as the cold steel touched his hand, startling him. He immediately quietened as he picked up the gadget and clutched it lovingly to his chest.

He had fallen into a light sleep. The weapon was still held tight between his hands, as dreams of home stirred his fractured soul. His thoughts drifted back to his family, and how his school teacher mother and office worker father had raised him and his sister with love. He was from a nice middle-class working family, showered in love and hugs, sometimes too much he often thought, but nevertheless always received. He dreamt of how his little sister, Kelly, had pestered him to play with her when all he wanted to do was hang out with his teenage friends. And when she wouldn't give in, he did; even when his friends laughed and mocked, he never let her down, and for this she adored him.

His nights out with his friends, the nightclubs and pubs as they staggered drunkenly from one venue to the next. The first proper girlfriend that he'd had, a brunette called Karen. What was he thinking as he fumbled clumsily with her bra strap on their first intimate date? Both giggling as the struggle turned into an epic fight with lace fabric and plastic clips. How they had laughed hysterically afterwards. Her laugh... he remembered her laugh. In this moment, he missed her terribly. Then there was the time when...

A loud bang struck the outside wall, waking him from the memories of his now lost life. He half opened his eyes, groggy. His heart fell once again as he realised where he was. It soon leapt into the roof of his mouth as the door panel began to glow.

'No, not yet, I'm not ready,' he cried. He juggled the weapon in his trembling hands, steadying it as best he could. With his back against the wall, his feet danced in cruel anticipation. He waited for the door to open... and waited, but it never happened. Why haven't they come for me, has something gone wrong?

As the silence continued, he remained on edge. He sat alert with the weapon poised, but still the door remained shut. He was aching to remove his jacket as the tightness had become increasingly uncomfortable, but he thought otherwise. Besides, it was too cold. Even though his jacket was thin, it was still an extra layer. I wonder if it's cold in here because they thrive in such conditions?

The triangle began to light, striking the mist. James jerked nervously, his head shooting from left to right as again he readied himself. Still holding the device, his right arm fell; the sound of the device hitting the floor waking him fully. He slowly climbed to his feet, the simplistic task becoming harder each time. The weapon shook heavily in his hand as he waited. Again, the door failed to open. He dropped back to his previous sitting position, using the wall as leverage to keep his body from collapsing. He growled at the stinging soreness that occupied his upper thighs as he moved. Looking down, his face contorted at the damp patch that had spread outwards from his crotch. He felt the area, hissing again at the chapped pain. 'Fucking hell,' he said in shame, realising that he had urinated while asleep.

He had by now given up on the smells in the room, including his own, as he was becoming accustomed to them. 'That's twice now that they haven't entered when the panel has been lit.' He sighed, smiling as his head fell back against the wall. 'You dozy twat! They haven't bloody entered the room because they've no intention of doing so,' he said. A grin of admiration spread across his weary features. 'Torture, it's all a form of torture.' He looked upwards and around the room. 'Did you read my mind you grey bastards, eh? I know what you're doing and it ain't working!' The truth was that it was working. He was finished, but he couldn't let them see, let them feel the weakness that seeped from every pore in his body.

He looked at the weapon once more, holding it close to his eyes; they hurt as they surveyed every part of the steel and its buttons. He liked playing with it, watching as the green electricity crackled and popped within the mist. It reminded him of a lightning storm, illuminating the clouds as it prepared to strike. He was going to miss the simple things in life.

His fingernails clicked as they caught the uneven flush rim of the small silver button. He brought the device further up into his eye-line for a closer inspection. 'Hmmm, Mark didn't want to push this button.' His fingers traced the slight curved bottom of the steel, rubbing it gently as he thought about whether or not to push the button. His childish enthusiasm got the better of him, he pushed. A six inch long spike thrust its way outwards from inside of the weapon with tremendous force, causing him to jump back. It was almost completely thin, though its base was wider, yet much smaller than the handle. He smiled as his eyes climbed the steel until they reached the sharp point.

'Nice,' he said as his nerves settled from the shock. He prodded the underside of his fingers with the point, which offered him some comfort in the form of tension release. Scraping the floor with it, he stabbed a nearby insect that made the mistake of entering his space. He held the point close to his face, watching curiously as the creature wriggled helplessly. He pulled the dying insect from the tip and thrust it into his mouth. He retched profusely as he crunched and chewed with speed before finally conceding defeat, and spitting the mangled legs and shell to the floor. He retched again as the remainders inside of his mouth left a nasty twang. 'I ain't doing that anymore.' Disgusted, he wiped the tip of the spike on his left sleeve. He looked at the purple guts that smeared his arm before rubbing over them with his right jacket cuff. Pressing the silver button, the spike sprung in reverse as it enclosed itself within the shaft.

He drifted again, this time dreaming of memories of home. At 11-years-old, his first day at Burnham Upper School in Opendale Road, Bucks, and the fear that followed. This fear served him in every aspect of his life from that day forwards. Whether meeting new people or starting a new job, the fear remained; it always reminded him of that first important day.

His dad dropped him off outside of the turquoise coloured gate. The place was huge compared to his Primary school. The old-fashioned box-like buildings appeared stacked upon one another as he stared out of the car window. 'Go on, son, you'll be okay,' his dad had said. James had fought his dad when he intervened, attempting to straighten his red, gold and royal blue tie. 'Just do your best, that's all you can do.'

He looked back at his dad who, sat in the family's 1970 bright red Vauxhall Viva, smiled. Embarrassed, he flicked a quick hand up as he gestured to say goodbye. He watched as his dad sped off. Turning, he felt daunted as he made his way through the gate and into the masses.

Suddenly, he was 18 and living in Shepherd's Bush, London. His expensive apartment was small but nice. The white walls had remained the same, even after his flatmates, Steve and Jenny, had moved in to share the overpriced cost.

Their nights at the Ginglik nightclub had become legendary over the last couple of years. The fun and laughs they'd had, were what life and friendships were about. The night that Steve was so drunk he fell down the steps to the club, and this was before they had got in, was talked about for months afterwards. Steve had stumbled halfway down the steps, hot footing it as he attempted to maintain his balance, only to have his fall cushioned by one of the door staff, a very big man at that, and not happy. Steve had laughed, and began mock swimming on top of the doorman's chest! The only thing that Steve got that night was a black eye from the incensed man.

'James, I love you,' said Catherine, his mother. The overpowering smell of her strong perfume, Tweed by Lenthéric, swamped his nostrils as she bent to kiss him on the cheek. Her hair, a greying bob, fell across his face before she cupped it gently with her small soft hands. 'Happy 16th birthday my baby boy.'

The perfume's dark green box was in the shape of a book. She had used it for as long as he could remember. It had fascinated him as a child; the white cameo head centred on the front cover looked elegant, rich.

He was five-years-old and he hid behind the discoloured white door frame. He watched on as her slender right middle finger delicately touched the miniature bottle's top, tipping it before dabbing the skin of her long elegant neck. She smiled into the mirror and winked as her blue eyes caught his tiny shadow hovering. He grinned back at her before running off.

'James, help me,' an eight-year-old Kelly had shouted. The older boys had pinned her against the wall; he stood scared as they slapped her around the head. Tears filled his eyes as the fear forced him into a 10-year-old coward. She came running into his arms when they released her.

He woke silently. His eyes welled as the memories were all too real. He still held onto the guilt over the last images. Even though it was a trivial event in his childhood, he was forever haunted by it. He could feel Kelly's little arms hold him tight, herself frightened as she hung on as though her life had depended on him.

I have a sister! He thought about her, excited at the fact that sections of his memory were returning. But he wondered where she was, and if she was safe? He was suddenly angry at himself, angry that he hadn't done more to pull her from the bullies' clutches. A tear descended from the corner of his eye. He knew that it was all a part of growing up, but still the images would never let him be. He pulled on tufts of his thin streaked hair as other faces drifted through his brain. 'My parents, my friends,' he whispered to himself, 'I can remember!'

The panel started to light up again. He gingerly climbed to his feet once more, holding the weapon with a lazy grip like a sleepy cobra waiting to strike. This time the door opened. He remained static for a minute before slowly venturing forward, towards the opening. The mist changed its aimless direction as it began to flow out and down the corridor. His hands shook as he held them out, ready for the fight. The haze cleared a little, making his vision easier. As he approached within a few feet of the door, it closed firmly with a whooshing force.

'Bastards!' he shouted. The insult echoed the room in a metallic tone as he realised that once again they were toying with him. 'I know what you're up to, not all of us humans are stupid!'

He moved back against the wall. Even though they were screwing with his head, he couldn't take the chance. He wanted to be ready, in case they did decide to come for him.

He sat for a while, trying to think. The dampness in his jeans hadn't dried much. It added a colder chill as his body reacted with another layer of goosebumps. All of a sudden, a screeching feedback-like sound pierced the room. He dropped the weapon as he clamped his hands over his ears, crying out as the violent noise drove through his senses. After several thunderous jolts it finally stopped. He lowered his hands cautiously as a metallic female voice spoke into the room.

'James. James, it's your mother. Are you okay, are you safe?' said the voice.

James leapt to his feet and looked around the room. 'What the...'

'James, we all love you and miss you. Your father and sister are here with me.'

He strolled round the room, looking upwards as he searched for a tannoy system of some type. But these were clever creatures, he didn't expect to find anything.

'Who is that speaking?' he raged with clenched fists. 'You're not my mother!'

'James, it's me, Catherine... your mother.'

'If it's really you then when were you born, what's your date of birth?'

'12th August, 1958. I was 37-years-old when I had you.'

He narrowed his eyes. Is this a trick? If it is, it's very good. He paused for several more seconds. 'Where are you now?' he asked casually.

'We are all here on the ship. But don't worry, son, we're safe and well. Kelly's here, she wants to talk to you.'

Another female voice entered the room, though this voice was harsher, less refined. 'James? Thank God you're okay. We've been worried sick about you.'

'Kelly, is that really you?' he asked. He was starting to believe.

'Yes, of course it's me! I wanted to tell you something. I wanted to tell you that I forgive you, and I don't blame you for freezing, for being scared when those bullies held me against the wall. It wasn't your fault, it's children being children that's all.'

James could feel the aggression rise in him. 'Nice try you fuckers, but not good enough! If you're going to fool me then don't play messages of shit like that, especially since I've just dreamt them.' He laughed aloud at their stupidity. 'I thought that you were supposed to be intelligent beings?' He ceased laughing as a strange thought suddenly occurred to him. How do they know what I've just dreamt? They must be monitoring my every thought, including this one!

'James, we love you. Your father wants to say hello,' the voice continued. 'James, are you there?'

He placed his hands back over his ears to silence the voices. He began crying hysterically as the emotion came flooding out of him, washing out all of the stress and fear. This was the final nail in his coffin. He knew that he was going to die here alone, there was no hint of escape, there never was.

He sat with his back against the wall, opposite to the door. His hands were rested on his kneecaps as he stared wide-eyed at the floor. The weapon hung from his fingertips, dangling as if about to fall at any second. For the first time since he had woken aboard this craft, he felt relaxed. There was no more pain in his toned torso, no more tightness in his shoulders, he felt... normal. The only feeling that hadn't changed was that of tiredness; he could easily fall asleep now and not wake for days. But what would be the point he thought, he would only come around to be faced with the same situation and set of problems. No, he would stay awake for as long as he could. He closed his eyes and let out a sigh. The thoughts raced through his mind before he reopened them.

'Mum, dad and Kelly. If you are listening to me now, I hope that you are safe. If not, then I pray to God to watch over you in the afterlife, I shall be joining you soon enough. I'm sorry for every single time that I made you all worry, or be concerned for my welfare, this I understand now. Kelly, I truly am sorry for not always being there for you. I hope that you can find it in your heart to forgive me; I know that you will, but I still have to ask. I love you all very much, as I do my dear friends; the laughs will continue in a better place. I love you all.'

The striking glow lit portions of the mist as the triangular panel lit up. James sat up straight as he heard the door open quickly. Two aliens walked through the opening, their eyes fixated on his calm being. He smiled as he focused on their shadowy frames that broke the mist's coiling patterns. He hauled himself up to his feet as the creature's approached. There they stood, silent as the swirls lovingly caressed their large heads and thin bodies as they looked down upon him with a burning hatred.

He removed his light jacket, letting it fall to the floor. He straightened himself to his full six foot height. 'Well, what are you waiting for?' he screamed. 'Come on then you fucking skinny grey freaks!' He held his arms at his side, careful not to reveal the weapon. 'You don't even understand what love and happiness are, do you? Your species is obviously incapable of experiencing it. This is what makes us different from you, better than you.'

The aliens' faces twisted with violent expressions as they moved in. James brought up his right arm in a flash and held the silver device against his throat. His heart beat rapidly, the sound of which could be heard pounding the walls of his ribcage. Black eyes looked on, enthralled as they measured the human's unusual behaviour.

'Checkmate,' he said in a low jittery voice.

The fear in his eyes betrayed the fighting posture that his body had taken. With that, he pushed the silver button on the bottom of the weapon. The long thin spike penetrated the soft flesh and jugular vein of his neck. The aliens took a step backwards, bemused as James' blood sprayed into the air like a thick red fountain. He dropped hard to his knees. The device was pulled from his neck as his arms lost their remaining strength. They crashed to the grating, his knuckles sliding in the oil and grime as he released the weapon.

The blood finished its rapid spurt, slowing to a sticky stream as it exited the five pence-sized puncture wound. He tried to speak, but couldn't; all he managed was a series of choking gulps as some of the blood ran down his throat. One of the aliens stepped forward and bent down. It stared into his eyes, fascinated as the dull brown colour became almost black as the life drained from the shell that held them. James fell sideways to the floor. The glimmer in his eyes became frozen in time, dead.

The alien continued to stare at the motionless body, studying it for a short while. It thrust down its arm, thumping its bony fist into the corpse's head. The jawbone snapped into two pieces, separating from the skull. It was followed by the left eye socket, struck with such force that the eye itself popped from the depressed fracture; it hung from its stalk, laying in a gruesome pose against the icy skin.

Both creatures looked at the blood and bones, mesmerised as the ivory pieces wallowed in the widening red pool. The alien's chest heaved heavily from the exertion as it regained its breath. It bent down and picked up the silver device that James had used. It held the weapon away from its body, and stared at the bloodied spike. It seemed intrigued as the liquid spiralled down towards the shaft. It pressed the button on the bottom of the steel, tilting its head as the spike speedily retracted. They each gripped an ankle, and proceeded to drag the body viciously out through the door.

Chapter 12

The Last Letter—James's Story

Thursday 11th April

I am writing this letter as there is not much time left. I hope that one day, if humanity survives, someone in the far future may be able to make more sense of why this has happened. Please forgive me if this is not written well, I am neither scholar nor expert.

The invasion officially began almost four months ago, on December 21st. All of the jokers who had scoffed at every "end of the world prophecy" (myself included), stopped rolling our eyes and started frantically praying.

At 9 p.m. the skies ripped open. Golden swirling patterns, like kaleidoscopes, spun hypnotically around the air. Hurricane strength winds blew in through the tears as the ships entered the dark stormy skies. Deafening booms thundered through the atmosphere, shaking the ground like enormous earthquakes and splitting the roads all over the city into pieces. The human race came to a standstill that night as we all watched in a state of confusion and awe, but mostly fear.

Television screens all over the world beamed out the images. The Presidents and Prime Ministers of the globe simultaneously spelt out the impending doom of an E.L.E. (Extinction Level Event). Piccadilly Circus was lit up like a Christmas tree, swamped by a sea of human light; the gathering of so many people was like seeing 10 of its New Year's Eve celebrations all rolled into one.

The British Prime Minister, addressed the country, loudly yet nervously. His face was white, drained of all life. I'll never forget the expression. It was genuinely like that of someone informing another of a relative's death, except that the death toll was to be potentially 70 million. Unfortunately the broadcasts came too late.

It turned out that the governments of the world had known that the 'Squawkers' (this is what we called them due to the horrible screeching sounds that occasionally they made had arrived two months earlier than when the invasion actually started.

According to our world leaders, along with the now common NASA footage that played on the news 24/7, they had first landed in the Ross Ice Shelf, in Antarctica.

Before it was destroyed, researchers at the McMurdo station (situated on the southern tip of Ross Island) had reported some strange occurrences in the atmosphere. For scientific purposes they had set up some small, simple camera equipment to document their experiments. This, unbeknownst to our invaders, had accidentally caught the moment they landed. Their subsequent activities were soon broadcast to NASA and the Pentagon by the terrified employees at McMurdo.

As we now know, the footage showed a rumbling rent in the skies over Ross Island. This was followed instantly by an enormous bright orange energy field, that engulfed the six massive ships in a dome-like shield. Each machine was at least the equivalent of 20 football pitches. The ships themselves were not your typical disc shaped crafts that one expected. Four of the giant machines were silver hexagonal crafts that were lit in a series of blinding white and amber lights. The other two were dark grey and rectangular, and covered in spiked weaponry. It seemed to NASA that the hexagonal ones were the "transporters", or "living quarters" that held the mechanics and scientists of their race. The remaining two, they theorised, were the military warships. These contained the soldiers for their security, and overall invasion plans.

This shield measured around 20 miles long and five miles high; it looked almost like liquid lava. The fizzy orange streams arced themselves like running water into the white icy sky before spreading outwards. It was a magnificent sight. The experts suggested that the South Pole and its magnetic field may have had something to do with why they landed on the Ice Shelf. They argued that because the South pole is cooler than the North pole, it aided them climatically in terms of their survival. This possibly gave them some clues to the origins of the grey Squawkers.

The film also showed some of the researchers from another nearby station, the Scott base. They managed to get close enough to the shield, and film portions of what was happening through the hazy, orange energy. The grainy camcorder footage showed the Squawkers building thousands more ships and weaponry, War of the Worlds style (for future reference: War of the Worlds—a novel by H.G. Wells).

We quickly saw their power as the skinny, seven-feet tall grey humanoid monsters went about their business. It was disturbing seeing and hearing these creatures. Their large black eyes and slits for mouths bore all the hallmarks of hardened invaders from any Hollywood science-fiction movie. It was frightening getting fleeting, shadowy glimpses of them, let alone their horrific instruments of war.

One of the female researchers within the group attempted to push a steel bar through the shield to test its security and scientific properties. Judging by their upbeat curiosity, I believe they thought that she would receive a small static jolt of electricity. Sadly though, the otherworldly energy disintegrated the bar into ashes, including her right arm up to her shoulder. The group watched helplessly as the charcoal dust scarred the crisp white ice. Shortly after, they were all violently caught and cruelly executed. After that happened every effort possible was made to communicate with the Squawkers, but all efforts were ignored.

Helicopters and fighter jets were constantly sent to protect the skies and surrounding lands. This included our own media invaders who threatened to stumble on to the events. The Americans even set up some small military bases on Ross Island, themselves housing soldiers and scientists. They were ordered to collect as much information as possible, still always cautious of the fate that had befallen the previous researchers. They managed to gather two months' worth of their own footage, though they failed in its attempts to learn anything really significant in terms of defeating them.

The leaders of the world had chosen to keep all of this a secret, in order to contain the mass levels of public panic and hysteria. Looking back on it now, I can completely understand and sympathise with their decision. The global governments had spent two months trying to come up with every imaginable solution for ensuring the survival of the planet and the human race. But as I said, it came too late; there was just simply not enough time. What would have been the point in telling us two months earlier anyway? At least millions died instantly, pain-free when the attacks came. We realised later that they were the lucky ones.

The 21st December, 9.00 p.m. was when the skies opened in a thunderous succession of tears in the space fabric. Thousands of flat triangle-shaped fighter ships, (NASA physicists agreed that they were transported through the same wormholes from Antarctica) three times the size of our jet fighters, spewed into the air all over the major cities of the world. These were followed by massive warships, similar to our own Naval Battleship aircraft carriers, except at least five times bigger. Even now, as I cast my mind back it seems weird, watching machines of that magnitude, floating effortlessly through the dazzling gold that lit up the night sky.

We were initially and naturally curious as these warships hovered, positioning themselves over every historical and important landmark of our time. This all changed within the hour as the Antarctica footage hit the Internet, going viral as the coordinated attacks began immediately all over the globe.

Our militaries managed to put up a small resistance. They even had some new weapons to use that were built especially in preparation for the assault; these were merely toys in comparison. Much of the advanced machinery that the aliens had built came straight out of any 21st century science fiction novel. From hovering tank-like machines, to weird creations that looked like giant metal grasshoppers with laser cannons. Then there were the water machines. These jumped in and out of the oceans, swimming like giant mechanical fish, and these were only a few of what they had built in Antarctica. The invisible bridges that extended from their ships and to our homes were the most chilling devices though. These allowed the creatures to abduct us from our lives, taking us out like the trash. It was disturbing to watch as people of all ages were marched out to the "carriers", for what purposes besides food, we still don't know.

It seems that they built their weapons here not only for convenience (the experts at NASA reckoned it was because their wormhole technology may have been limited), but were also built specifically to combat the terrains, properties, and different military elements of our world. Experts concluded that the Squawkers had studied all life on the planet. They agreed that they had designed their machines accordingly, to mimic the characteristics of certain insects or animals that best benefitted them when hunting their prey. In this instance the "prey" being us.

Our brave heroes were virtually all incinerated from the skies before dawn. Fighters dropped out of the sky like fiery flies as black smoke engulfed the early morning air. Battleships and warships were sunk like heavy stones in a rippling pond, crushed silently by the pressure as they fell to the bottom of the oceans. Missiles and rockets didn't even make a dent on most of the enemy machines. We didn't stand a chance.

The ground armies fared no better in their wars. Millions of soldiers, from all military walks of life, littered the streets like forgotten garbage. Defeat thickened the atmosphere, it was horrendous. Then came the news and video footage reported from around the world, and their respective fights.

Huge monuments of human endeavour were shattered in the blink of an eye. After all, most countries still only tolerated each other for personal or political gain. Though seeing the Eiffel tower in Paris turned into great falling chunks of scrap metal, well, that did force a tear in many a man's eye. Brazil's "Christ the Redeemer" statue in Rio was burnt to dust, which brought thousands into the streets in mass prayer. These were the first landmarks to go, others quickly followed.

Those who survived the initial invasion were swiftly rounded up like cattle. They were lined up in the streets and obliterated to ashes for the whole world to see. This included children of all ages, wiped from the face of the Earth as though they had never been born. The only ones to survive seemed to be the elderly. If you were over seventy, you were led away. We were never sure why. Again, experts suggested that the elderly were deemed not a threat, and taken away to be used as food, but again this was never proven.

I never knew what happened to my family. The initial attacks caused millions of tonnes of debris to block the streets and roads across the entire city. Large sections of the motorways were destroyed instantly. We think that this was because they wanted to cut off any means of escape, to prevent the population of London from seeking sanctuary outside of the city.

I chose to get out from my rented flat in Shepherd's Bush, within two hours. I don't know where my flatmates were at the time, or if they are even still alive (Steve Broomfield and Jenny Carter), but I pray that they are safe somewhere.

After seeing the smoke climbing high from the Shepherd's Bush tube station, half a mile away, I chose a different route. It was heart wrenching, exhausting as I clawed and fought my way through the screaming human traffic. It had become just as dangerous on land now as it was in the skies.

It took several hours, but I managed to survive the trek amidst the attacks and the rioting. I made it to my parents' house the following night in Burnham, Buckinghamshire. Their street, Coalman's Way, and most of the adjacent estates, had been demolished. I tried to help frantic old neighbours and friends search the rubble for our families after the initial attacks had quietened, but as far as we could dig we found nothing. I never knew if they managed to survive the first wave of attacks or not.

As for my sister, Kelly, I have no idea if she escaped. I think she was on the underground at the time of the invasion. She had texted me earlier in the day about a gig she was going to that night in Covent Garden. A group of teenagers had told me that most of Liverpool Street underground station had collapsed in on itself. Hopefully she made it out in time, but she hasn't contacted me since, so I'm assuming she's dead.

Of the military personnel who managed to escape the onslaught, most made it underground into the sewer systems. There, they formed alliances and small resistance groups in an attempt to survive. We were glad of their efforts as they helped us to get organised. Their experience and knowledge turned our groups (who mostly consisted of lost loners like myself) into small armies and operations. Without them we would have been dead inside of two weeks, especially when the ground invasions began.

Those who managed to escape the onslaughts in the skies, and then the ground invasions, and who didn't manage to find us underground were deemed the walking dead. The Squawkers sprayed the oceans, rivers, and crops with chemicals unknown to man. These killed everyone and everything who dared to drink or eat from them. Add to this the stench and the disease that followed as the millions of the dead began to decompose, it wasn't pretty. The Squawkers seemed to delight in any form of death that the human race suffered. It didn't matter to them, except that they wanted every death to be the worst, most horrific case that they could conceive. Even those, who by some miracle managed to evade all these obstacles, eventually turned on each other for what food and clothing remained (rumours of cannibalism were rife, but personally I never saw any evidence of this). Nothing survived up top on land.

We always had small glimmers of hope knowing that the world's leaders were hidden away somewhere in their secret bunkers. We prayed that they were with the top military brasses, planning their big offensives, and our overall survival.

The military even brought in psychic mediums in an effort to tele- pathically read the minds of any captured enemies. Confidence was high when they said they could drag vital intelligence on any attacks from the creatures, or at least find out why they were here. It failed miserably. Other glimmers soon faded as we found out that the worm- holes the Squawkers used were not only for their ships and weaponry, but also for themselves. They could transport any number of their race to any part of the world, anytime they wanted.

This was particularly soul destroying on the day last week when all hopes were finally lost. The world collectively exhaled, as every tele- vision set that still worked broadcast what is left of the news channels.

Military units of Squawkers had been transported to a minority of secret government bunkers around the world, including us, Great Britain, and the United States of America. There we watched, trans- mitted all over the world live by these sadistic invaders, the sicken- ing execution of our Prime Minister. This was swiftly followed by the most powerful man on the planet, the President of the United States of America. Slain in the streets, left like dog's shit in the gutter, our leaders and spirits were crushed. I fear it is only a matter of days now before the rest of the world's leaders are rounded up and forced to share the same fate.

As for the Royal Family? I can only assume that they were shipped out to their safe bunkers the day that the aliens had landed in Antarc- tica. I did hear that Princes William and Harry were involved in our country's offensive. It was said that William led squadrons of jet fight- ers during the many dogfights in the skies, while Harry had his own battalion that fought hard on the ground. If they are still involved, or even alive, I don't know.

Because of these intrusions we now have to be even more alert as they can appear at anytime, anywhere. We place down tin foil and tal- cum powder in areas of our sewer hideouts not frequently used. These are rigorously checked for strange footprints and markings several times daily. It has proved effective at knowing if the Squawkers have entered our safe houses at any point. This gives us the chance to sweep for any technology not recognised by human eyes. We have to do this as they constantly use bugs in the hope of learning vital intelligence concerning the bigger resistance groups. If we find any we move on, but they are not stupid. Again, this simple test won't last, but for now it gives us a slight peace of mind, however small.

All over the world there are whispers of these resistance groups, though our numbers deplete rapidly by the day. It is thought that there are only around 1-1.5 million humans left on the planet, we are a dying breed. Every couple of days small groups of us go on food and pharmaceutical runs. We search everything from abandoned houses to litter bins, desolate shops to broken down vehicles, all in the hope of finding any nourishment and medicine that we can get our hands on. Even then we always come home minus some of the numbers we went out with. There are always alien scouts, or some form of trap waiting for us. They have destroyed everything in their path, and we still don't even know why they are here. All we know is that they are intent on our complete annihilation.

I feel sick as I write this… my throat burns from another acid reflux. I hope I haven't contracted any disease from any chemical-laced food that we found recently. My hands have been shaking slightly for the last few hours, but I put this down to fear, stress, and hunger.

When the attacks first happened we all saw the hatred and ruthlessness that accompanied them. I thought that I would welcome my death, hopefully pain free if possible. But now that the human race is on the brink of total destruction I feel incredibly angry.

Our species is almost gone. Shall I disappear without a whimper? After all, who cares when you're dead, right? Yet the other half of me wants to fight. Fight to protect every great piece of music or song ever composed, to protect every great book ever written, to protect every fantastic movie ever made. I want to protect every great and wonderful memory every person has ever had or shared. How dare they attack our homes and destroy our lives, and everything that we, as a race stand for! But who am I? An insignificant speck of dirt who merits no worth to these monsters.

I can hear heavy rumbles above the ground. I think it may be an approaching unit of Squawkers and their machines. The rumblings feel like they're getting closer. I don't think this is a scouting mission as I can hear the sound of marching feet. There must be many as their footsteps are thundering over the humming whirs of the machinery. There must be hundreds of them, otherwise they would have energised directly here. Pieces of dirt and concrete are starting to crack overhead under the oncoming weight, falling like grey hail stones.

I can now see down the long stretch of sewer from one of the many makeshift offices here, and all I see is intense fear. Every face I glance at has the petrified look of "is this the end?" painted across it. Some of the younger children are trembling badly as they try to shield their heads from the concrete rain. Others are vomiting what little they have left in their malnourished bodies.

I have just been sick again and the sweat is pouring off me. I can hear explosions close by, I think they have found us and breached the compound. I can hear my fellow humans screaming in agony as they try to fight. I'm scared, shaking as I hear the children crying. Our gun fire is pathetic, no match for the extreme alien weaponry as the noise gets louder, closer.

Oh no, I can see gold swirls materialising everywhere... they are making me dizzy as I stare at them. They are here. I can see Squawkers stepping out of thin air down the tunnel, there are lots of them. I'm very frightened, but it's pointless trying to run, I'm trapped anyway. If there is a God, I hope he's waiting to welcome us home.

Oh Christ, there's a blinding white light beginning to flood the tunnel.

I'm sorry about the stains that may blot some of this letter, but I can't stop the tears. I gaze at them, hypnotised as I watch the blue ink blend with the wetness as all around me begins to illuminate. But it's okay, the words that I write shall linger long after, whatever form they may take. My heart aches as I know that the end of me, the human race, and everything we have ever known is at a violent end. I finish this letter with the fact that I now understand why we are so special. No matter what anyone has ever done in life, good or bad, know that as a unique species, I forgive you. But most importantly, I love you all.

Yours truly,

James Robert Jones Jr

Age: 19, occupation: human, resistance (K. I. A.)

Dear reader,

We hope you enjoyed reading *Blurred Vision*. Please take a moment to leave a review, even if it's a short one. Your opinion is important to us.

Discover more books by Chris Botragyi at
https://www.nextchapter.pub/authors/chris-botragyi

Want to know when one of our books is free or discounted? Join the newsletter at http://eepurl.com/bqqB3H.

Best regards,
Chris Botragyi and the Next Chapter Team

You could also like:

Cuttin' Heads by D.A. Watson

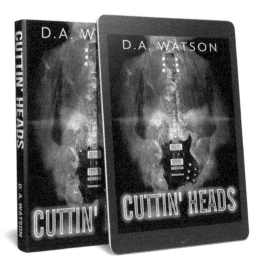

To read the first chapter for free, please head to:
https://www.nextchapter.pub/books/cuttin-heads

Bibliography

Kurtus, R, School for Champions, (2015), Centripetal and Centrifugal force (modified by myself), http://www.school-for-champions.com/

Blurred Vision
ISBN: 978-4-86752-661-3

Published by
Next Chapter
1-60-20 Minami-Otsuka
170-0005 Toshima-Ku, Tokyo
+818035793528
5th August 2021

Lightning Source UK Ltd.
Milton Keynes UK
UKHW010102070722
405488UK00001B/20